The Vow

by

Kristina M.

Cover Photography by Zsofia Balassa
Editing by Paige Lawson

DEDICATION

To my husband to be who I love very much and can't wait to marry.

CONTENTS

CHAPTER 1

It is the warmest day of summer. There is not even a single cloud in the sky or a little breeze to cool the air. Even if it rains, it wouldn't matter. It is simply the best day of our lives.

"You may kiss the bride," – says the master of ceremonies, and the only thing you can hear is the cheering of the guests in the background. I look over the crowd at all the young faces. Most of the girls have tears in their eyes. Their boyfriends holding their tissues to wipe their tears away. The ladies are always touched by weddings. The gentlemen clap and look at their friend with proudness.

As we walk in front of all the guests and they start throwing white rose petals at us, I remember the first time I walked down the aisle. It seemed for a second like it was just yesterday, but it was decades ago. The crowd follow us to the restaurant where everybody looks for their places and judges the seating plan.

The restaurant looked better than ever. After my divorce with Nate, I got full ownership over the place and redecorated the interior, which is up to date with the newest trends every few years. I spent a lot of money on the design. It was already three Michelin Stars, and I couldn't afford to lose the place. It is now one of the few elegant places, where the prices are not overpriced and a lot of locals come. During Summer, every Friday and Saturday is always fully booked with weddings or birthday celebrations. There are even dates in the calendar that have a long waitlist and are booked years in advance. The kitchen received an extension, and instead of keeping a wall between the guests and the kitchen, we created a glass wall, so everybody can see how the food is made. The number of tables stayed the same as before, however, the terrace is bigger. We added around fifteen additional tables on the new open-area above the cliff, and in some parts, even a glass floor. Those tables are only used on very busy nights, as not many people dare to sit there. For me, it was even more spectacular to have the glass below my feet. There were only rare nights when the restaurant wasn't fully booked. Even though I have a sales team, the place practically runs itself.

When I look around the restaurant, I notice Nate on the side and smile at him. He has his charming looks even now. The subtle white strands of hair and beard make him look even more charming. The grey suit with the pink napkin and rose really brings out his nice eyes. He throws me a smile, and raises a glass. I walk over to him.

"Nice to see you, Nate" – I kiss his cheek and smile.

"You look amazing as always, Tess." – He smiles and places his hand on the back of the woman standing with her back towards us. She turns and smiles at me like she already knows who I am.

"Oh, Tess. Hi! Congratulations" – she leans in and hugs me.

"Thank you! I am sorry, but I must have missed your name."

"I am Sasha. Sorry. I heard so much about you from Nate. It seemed to me like I already know you." – Nate places his hand on her waist.

"Tess, this is the lady I told you about who stole my heart." – if the hand isn't obvious enough, this introduction sure is. His plus one. She is as tall as Nate; her figure is like a model. Tall, long legs and the dress is grey like his suit with an open back. There isn't a gram of meat on her back; it's all bones and muscles. She has the perfect figure. Her brown hair is tied up in a nice big donut bun with a few pieces of hair curled on the side. Her blue eyes are like Nates and her nude lipstick balances the dark make up on her eyes.

"Nice to meet you, Sasha. Sorry, it was a long day, and I couldn't remember your name. I am glad to hear you make Nate so happy." – I place my hand on Nate's shoulders, smile at them and walk away to greet the other guests.

After a few 'Hello. How are you?'-s I get tired and make my way outside for a bit of fresh air. I walk to the corner table, where Nate and I had our first date. It was the first time I saw this view and fell in love with this place. I place my elbows on the side of the fence and hold my chin with my hands, and just stare at the sky.

"How is it possible that one of the most important people of this wedding is here alone staring at the sky and not inside?" – says a voice behind me, which made me turn in that direction.

"Just wanted to get some air," – I reply and start to walk back inside. – "Are you coming?" – I turn and ask.

"I'm coming, Boss." – Ramos smiles and starts walking towards me. We dance ourselves into the crowd and join the guests in the games and drinking. Ramos has his wonderful smile and blue suit, which emphasizes his green eyes. He is a beautiful sight, as always.

When we come in, it is already time to cut the cake and play some games. It feels the same as last time, as time is much faster on this one day than any other day. After the first dance, it is just a party until the morning. At the end, there is only a few of us staying and making our last moves on the dancefloor, and soon we are all on the way home.

Mom and her husband are already quite old, but they are one of the biggest party people I know. They were just dancing the whole night and sat down only for a refill. Steve and Nicole are helping the catering team to be on track with everything. Their children, Vincent and Jessie, are already with their friends, waiting for the oldies to leave so they can enjoy the party. Lara was so excited the whole day that I think she even got the chance to enjoy the night.

When we arrive home, it feels so empty. The flat is quiet after the whole party atmosphere. It feels strange and unfamiliar. I take off my high heels, which have been killing my feet for a few hours. I am not young anymore. This is the first time I realize that. I am not the 20-year-old Tess anymore. I need to take it slow. Before jumping into the bed, I take a glance at the bedroom door from Lara.

"Are you coming?" – says the voice from the bedroom.

"I'll be right in. Give me a second." – I turn on the light in Lara's room. It's empty. Everything is as she left it. The pink walls that we painted when she was a teenager, the posters of her favorite bands, and her bed is still warm. She spent her previous night still sleeping here, but now, she is a grown-up already. I sit on the bed and lay down for a while. I remember the first time I tucked her in. I look around and see the mess in her cupboard, which she never cleans up. Clothes are still on the floor. Her books from university piled up. Some stuffed animals looking at me from the window. She still left a few of her favorites, even though she promised to take them with her anywhere she goes. Every single piece in the room has a memory of an event or a person in her life.

"She is doing alright." – says the voice standing at the door.

I couldn't move. I just lay there with closed eyes as tears ran down my cheeks.

"I know." – I reply quietly. When I open my eyes, he is sitting on the edge of the bed and looking at me with a cheesy smile on his face.

"You know. I remember your room was similar to this when we were young. Just you were allowed to bring boys, and she isn't." – he says.

"Hey. That's not fair. I let her. It's just she has to be picky and not let anybody close to her heart." - I sit up on the bed and take Lara's pillow in my hands.

"You are a great mother. Don't worry. It was a great day and a big day for us today. We should enjoy it and not cry about something else." – he stands up and gives me his hand.

I place my hand in his and follow him. Before we leave the room, I look at the room one last time and turn off the lights and make my way to the bedroom.

I take a deep breath and close my eyes. It was one of the longest dreams I ever had. I went back in time to the moment it was Lara's first day at school. The first day I realized how time goes in a blink of an eye. The next time I opened my eyes, I was over 50 and having the man of my dreams wake up beside me.

CHAPTER 2

It was 6 a.m. when the alarm went on, and I jumped up in the bed. It was the first day of school. I ran out to the kitchen prepared a cup of coffee and breakfast for Lara. Her favorite was Coco Pops with milk. She ate that almost every day, without ever getting bored of it. I went to Lara's room to wake her up. When I opened the door, she was already wide awake, sitting on the bed.

"I am ready, mommy. Let's go.' – she said with her cute voice. She tried to make her hair smart and put on some pink lipstick she had as a toy. Her eyes were still sleepy, but she was ready. She was always up earlier than the alarm whenever I told her we had to wake up early the next day. It was amazing to see, as I was never a morning person. The first day of my school was more of a disaster. I remember the huge traffic, Steve and I still sleepy in the back of the car and listening to the radio on the way to school.

"Come on, sweetie. Let's get you dressed, and we can go". – I opened her cupboard and took out the dress I'd prepared for her. It was a white shirt with a cute squared skirt. We bought the black school shoes and little socks. I combed her hair and put it to the side. She never liked it when I did too much hairstyle. She only wanted me to comb it and leave it as it is.

"Get some breakfast and I'll get ready." – she jumped up on the kitchen counter and ate her breakfast while I turned on a cartoon to keep her entertained while I got ready.

I went to pick up a pair of jeans and shirt, combed my hair, brushed my teeth and was ready to leave. When I got back to the kitchen, I heard somebody turning the key at the entrance. Before I got there, the doors opened, and Nate was standing there. I gave him a set of keys in case of an emergency, but he used it too often to come whenever he wanted.

"Daddy!" – Lara screamed and ran over to Nate's arms.

"Emergency keys. You remember?" – I looked at him.

"It's her first day. It's an emergency." – he smiled and cupped Lara's face and gave her a big kiss on the forehead.

"Let's go. We shouldn't be late the first day."

"I'll drive," – Nate said, and we were out. I rolled my eyes and locked up the apartment.

We were in the car, and Lara talked about all the friends

she was going to make the first day. She even knew the names in advance and told us she wouldn't be friends with blondes as mommy said they are mean. I was glad she was paying attention to me, but now I actually didn't want her to. When we got to the school, the parking lot was full of parents running around and chasing their kids.

As I was keen on Lara going to the same school as I did, we got special rates and paid only half of the tuition. Nate was not happy with the decision as he thought she would be a snob, but he would appreciate it in time. Lara was getting quiet as we got out of the car, and saw all the kids running around. She took my hand, and I squeezed it. In the classroom, she chose the first row next to a Chinese boy. She smiled at him, and they both just stared blankly.

"It's going to be a great day. You will find some friends in a blink of an eye. Just be yourself." – I kissed her on the forehead, and Nate followed.

"Don't go, mommy. Stay…" - she took my hand and held me close to her.

"Mommy will be here soon to pick you up." – I gave her another kiss, and with that Lara's eyes were filled with tears. She jumped up from her seat and clung onto my neck. I hugged her and pushed her away so I could see her face. I cleaned her tears and smiled at her.

"I love you, honey. You are so brave. Don't cry." – Lara's lips were still sad, but then she looked up and saw a friendly old lady stare at her.

"How are we doing here?" - the lady said and exchanged a look with Lara and me. – "What's your name, darling?"

"Lara" – with that, she sat back on the chair and let go of my neck. I stood up and took a step back and went beside Nate.

"Nice to meet you. I am Ms. Gayle. Would you like to come with me and I can show you some toys we have here?" – she held her hand out, which Lara took immediately, and they were off. The lady turned and gave us a nod that we could leave.

Nate and I ran out, so Lara wouldn't notice, but she was so busy already that she didn't even turn. She started playing with a few other kids, and soon Ms. Gayle told them to have a seat, and they would start the lesson. We stayed for a bit to see if it was alright and then left. On the way out, I saw a paper for the parent committee, and signed up as a volunteer.

"So this means you will pick her up?" – Nate looked at me.

"No, it means I am glad to help. Let's go, we have to set up the new menu."

Nate and I drove to 'Josephs Dream' and then went our own way. We shared many rides to work, where we discussed the schedule for Lara or some investment ideas for the restaurant. We kept everything really professional. Every month once, we had a family lunch at the restaurant to show Lara that we were getting along. We would then cook together and teach Lara a few tricks in the kitchen. She was quite a talent for her age, but as her mother, she loved the patisserie most.

It was four years since we me and Nate had split up. Lara and I moved to a nice flat with a big terrace. It wasn't that far away from the restaurant, so I went for a long walk or took a bike to work if Lara was not coming with me. Lara and I both loved the apartment, and we were planning to stay there for the long term. When you entered, you had a big spacious living room with a direct connection to the kitchen and dining room. One whole wall was made from glass, which would take you to the terrace. It was so light the whole day in the flat that we rarely turned up any lights during the day. On the left was a guest bedroom with a bathroom. Directly next to it was Lara's room. Since we moved to the apartment, she never changed anything in the room except her bed size. It was still pink walls with white furniture. The only thing she wanted additional was a TV in her room, which I promised to give her when she is ten and has good grades. Opposite her room, just on the other side of the glass wall, was my bedroom and the bathroom next to it, which both of us used. The guest toilet was sperate next to the entrance. The whole apartment was in grey, and green design, except the bedrooms, which were a brown and beige mixture. After my bad experience with the help of others, I designed the whole apartment alone, and I loved that part the most. Moving in was a mess, and it was still the period I didn't want to hear Nate's name.

Nate moved to a smaller flat, which was more like his old one. Bachelor flat with an empty fridge, except when Lara was there. She had her own little room, and he spent more money on that room than any other furniture in the flat. Everything was from IKEA, except hers. She picked her own things, and as she had good taste, most of them were not the cheapest. Nate and I had a good agreement, and he got quite a nice salary to pay his loan and put something aside. I wanted him to open something of his own later and do his own kitchen again, but he loved 'Josephs's Dream' too much and didn't seem as he was planning to leave.

It was 2 p.m. and time to pick up Lara.

"Would you like to come, or should I pick her up and bring her here" – I asked Nate.

"I am pretty busy. Can you bring her here, and I'll make dinner and let you get back to your thing until I am with her."

I turned and took his keys and went to the school to pick her up. When I got there, I checked the list of people who signed up for the parent committee again to see if I knew somebody. I saw Joanna on the list, but she was president. I didn't know the rest of the people, but I saw it was mostly mothers except one.

When I got to the classroom, Lara was laughing with one of the boys.

"Lara" – I said, and she turned and ran towards me. – "Are you ready to go?" – she jumped and hugged me like we hadn't seen each other in ages.

"Yes." – she replied and ran back to pick her bag and wave to the other boy she spoke with.

We made our way to the car when I saw that Nate's car

was scratched on the side and a young man stood next to it swearing.

"Hey. Hey. Children. Please." – I walked over, and he turned and stopped.

"I am sorry. My phone rang, and I didn't pay attention and…." – he started before I interrupted.

"It's alright. It's my ex-husbands. He probably deserves it." – I smiled and opened the door for Lara to get in.

"I am Tess. Are you here to pick up your child or just to hit cars?" – I closed the door and turned towards him.

"To pick up my son. I am Ramos. Nice to meet you." – he put his hand out, and only then I saw he had green eyes like the grass. It was an interesting combination, as he had dark brown hair, darker skin color and a big beard.

"Spanish?" – I replied.

"Was it the accent or the name that gave me away?"

"The bad driving" – I opened the door, smiled and sat in the car to drive away.

Ramos was standing there and waved goodbye to us. He was very charming with his accent. For some reason, his name sounded very familiar, but I didn't remember where from. Maybe we worked together earlier. On the way to the restaurant, Lara couldn't stop speaking about Ms. Gayle and Jake. In her voice, I could hear she was very excited to go back tomorrow, which is a good sign. From the stories she told me, I realized Jake is the boy with whom she spoke with at the end. When we got to the restaurant, Nate was already outside waiting with open arms for Lara to rush to him, which she did as soon as I stopped the car. I took her things from the car and made my way inside to pick up the rest of my belongings and go home. Nate already packed my dinner for a take away, which he placed beside my bag. I kissed Lara and handed Nate his car keys.

"Tell me tomorrow what you did with the car. Thanks for the pickup."

"Wasn't me. See you, tomorrow sweetie. Be good with daddy." – I walked away with no further discussion.

I walked home and used the time to call Brian to catch up.

"Hello stranger." - he picked up.

"When will I get to see you?"

"I am free now. Want to talk to you about something." - I

paused and wondered what was wrong.

"Come over, I'll be there in 15 minutes." – we hang up and I buy some snacks on the way home.

We arrived at the same time to the apartment, and he helped me carry up the bags to the apartment. On the way up, I told him how happy I was that Lara had an easy first day at school and how this guy hit Nate's car. He mostly liked that part, as he still hated him for everything he had done. When we got in, I took the food out and a bottle of wine to drink.

"So, what's up with you? Are you alright?" – I asked.

"Yeah. I have a bit of an issue with my apartment." – he stopped and poured a big glass of wine. – "You know the renovations they did last year on the roof?" – I nodded. – "Well, it was bloody expensive, and I thought it is all done, but then recently the walls started getting wet, and I thought it was just some pipe problem."

"Did you check it out?" – I asked worriedly.

"Of course. They said it was done badly from the start, and they have to re-do the whole apartment from the beginning." – he bent on the kitchen island and put his hand on his forehead. I could hear in his voice something else was bothering him.

"What's your plan? Are you going to sell or move somewhere to rent for a while?" – he just starred and didn't respond. – "Hey. It's going to be alright. I have an idea for you." – I walked over and placed my hand on his shoulder, and smiled at him.

"Why don't you stay with Lara and me in the guest bedroom until you have it sorted? As rent, you can pick up Lara sometimes or go shopping for groceries." – I pulled his face up with my hands and kissed him on the cheek and turned back to the vegetables.

"I can't accept that. You have your little girl here, and what if I bring someone home or you have some guy here?"

"First of all, I don't have time for guys. I haven't had sex in ages, and you can do it in quiet and nobody will notice. Probably you can crash at the girl's place, only if you don't pick up some teenager again." – he walked towards me and hugged me.

"What would I do without you? Thanks, Tess. I will be the best Godfather to Lara and help you with whatever."

"You can start with cutting the vegetables instead of just drinking." – we laughed, and he took the knife and started cutting.

We spent the whole evening planning how to move his belonging and if I had enough storage space in the basement to keep the rest of the things. His furniture would stay at his place, and he would use what I had, which was in excellent shape. At the end, we fell asleep on the couch with wine and food still lying all over the living room. We both woke up to the doorbell. I stood up and helped myself to my feet by holding his knee.

"Good morning. Wait here." – I opened the door, and it was Nate and Lara. Lara was like an eagle. She always saw everything first and ran towards it like she saw her next pray.

"Brian." – She shouted and ran towards him. – "Are you here to play?" – she looked at him with big eyes and already took his hand to walk him into her room. He followed and smiled at me. I turned back to Nate, whose face looked confused.

"We agreed. No relationships until she is older. What are you doing?" – he looked angry.

"Yes, he is a friend. We drank a bit and fell asleep on the couch. Alright, daddy?" – I showed him the way to the kitchen and then thought it would be the perfect chance to tell him about Brian moving in.

"Nate." – he stopped and turned. – "There is something you should know. Brian will move in with us."

"He will what?" – he shouted

Brian came out the moment Nate raised his voice.

"Hey man, chill. I have a plumbing problem, and Tess offered for me to stay here until it's fixed." – he interrupted and tried to be as polite as possible, even though he hated him.

"It was my idea, and you have nothing to say. You are not living here, plus Lara loves to play with Brian. He will help with her school in exchange." – I turned to Nate, but he was still staring at Brian.

"I don't like it, but you don't care what I say. Just don't let your stupidity get in the way of Lara." – he stopped and walked to Lara's room to get her ready for school.

I shook my head.

"I'll get going to get everything settled. Thanks for everything. I'll call you when I have the date to move." – I didn't even reply, only nodded. I went to change and get a shower while Nate prepared Lara. When I got out, both of them were standing at the door, ready to go.

"Today, I am driving." – I took my keys, and we were ready for another day at school.

The drop-off was going smoothly. Two kisses, and she was off to play with Jake. She seemed to like him a lot. Nate and I went back to the restaurant, and a few hours later, I had my first Parent Committee meeting. Joanna was the only other one there when I arrived.

"Hey. How are you?" – I hugged her.

"I am so happy to see you joined. I needed some support. There are so many crazy women here. How was the first day?" – she smiled and started to place the chairs next to each other.

"Oh. I am looking forward to it. Let me help you." – I joined her in the arranging. – "It was easier than I thought. The teacher, Ms. Gayle, was so nice. Today we only got two kisses, and that was it."

"Wait. We? Nate and you?" – she stopped

"Yeah. It's only at the beginning. I don't want people to think we are a thing. Guess what? His car was scratched by a hot dad yesterday." – we laughed.

"Which hot dad?" – she asked as the door opened, and a few people walked in.

"Actually him." – the only man in the room was Ramos. The rest was moms. Joanna looked at me and gave me an approving look after checking him out. She then walked over to greet the rest of the team, and I stayed back to finish with the chairs.

"Do you need a hand?" – a voice from the back asked, and as I turned, I saw Ramos standing there. He and his gorgeous green eyes staring at me.

"I'm alright. What are you doing here with so many women?" – I asked while I finished and started to walk towards the group.

"I want to know everything what is happening around my son."

"What about your wife? It's usually a woman thing."

"Divorced." – he responded calmly.

"Sorry. Me too if it makes you feel better." – I smiled at him.

"Group, please have a seat. We will start the meeting soon." - Joanna interrupted. – "I am Joanna. My kids are in the 5th and 3rd grade. I have been part of this committee since the first day. We are all here to make the school life of our kids better. We will plan all events arranged by the school and additional activities, such as babysitting or play nights, which are made outside of the school. From my experience, the first day, we have around 15 motivated moms and sorry dads, but after the third meeting, there is only five or six who stay and help." - she looked around, and it seemed she already knew who would stay and go.

We went through all the Events planned for the first year and the most important things we have to do. All of us did a short introduction to who we are and how much time we had spare to help. Ramos was a freelancer and quite motivated to help. Two other single moms lived from divorce money and had a lot of spare time. Both of them had their eyes on Ramos. By the end of the meeting, five decided to leave the committee. The two single moms, Ramos, Joanna and two other moms, including me, stayed.

"For play nights, we usually do pairs and only if both sides of the party are busy, we ask somebody else to help out." – The two singles starred at Ramos. One raised her hand to speak and offer her pair, but before they did, Joanna added. – "The pairing is made according to what your children like and with whom they like to play with. As I did a little research, the pairs will be the following way. Jackie and Julie. Natalie and Jessie. Tess and Ramos will be in pair with me. Jake and Lara are basically always together, and as my pair left, I will join you. Thank you all for being here. See you next week."

Jackie and Julie exchanged a mean look and looked at me like they were going to kill me.

"Jake is your son?" – I turned to Ramos

"I could ask you the same. Jake was talking about Lara the whole day. I wanted to check her out today." – he smiled

"Well. Play nights are good for the kids."

"Maybe we can both be there on the play nights." - he winked and grab his jacket, and left to pick up Jake.

I looked at Joanna, who was watching us from the other side of the room.

"What are you up to?" – I asked her with crossed arms

"Nothing. Just two nice people with kids the same age are by accident in the same group." – she made a cheeky smile

"Give me your list."

"No. Come on, Tess. Let's go." – before she could leave, I took the paper from her hand and saw the pairs she wrote up were completely different than what she'd pretended to read up. I looked at her with a big smile and shook my head. When we walked out to the foyer, Ramos was standing there with Jake and Lara and looking at me through the crowd.

"Hey, sweetie." – I bent down to kiss Lara, who jumped at me for a big kiss. – "Did you introduce yourself to Jake's dad?" – she nodded and went over to hold Jake's hand as they started to walk out of school.

"Do you want to hold my hand as well?" – Ramos asked

"Stop it. Come let's go home."

"I am not ready to go with you. Maybe another time, before that, I want to get to know you."

"I didn't mean it like that. Sorry" - I looked down shyly and followed Lara towards the exit.

When we got to our car, Ramos was parking next to us.

"I hope you didn't scratch my car."

"I paid extra attention." – he opened the door for Jake and went to the driving side, which was next to my door as he parked the other way around. I opened the door, took a business card out of my bag and handed it to him.

"Call me if you want a play night." – I smiled and turned.

"I definitely will."

I didn't wait long for him to call me. When I arrived home, I already had a friend request on Facebook, and he followed me on Instagram. When I finished feeding and preparing Lara for bed, I had time to get some work done and prepare for the next week's Parent Committee meeting. The only problem was that I didn't do anything of it.

Lara sleeping? Are you free for a chat?

I stared at the message for a while and wondered whether I should write back or not. I checked my emails, and most of them were done already by my assistant. I went back to the message and started typing.

You know it's their time. What are you up to?

I called my mom to tell her about the first day at school and ask how she was. We still kept our tradition to speak every day, just now it was extended to late hours. After, I wrote Nicole and Steve about the weekend plan to take the kids hiking, then I went to take a bath. When I sat down in the bath, my phone started to ring. I picked it up without looking who it is.

"Hello?"

"Hi. Bad timing?" – Ramos replied.

"Oh shit. Sorry. I didn't see who was calling. May I call you back later? I am in the bath."

"That means you have time to talk. If you call later, I will be sleeping. We can talk another time."

I paused and thought that later I will probably sleep.

"It's good now. Sorry. I had a long day."

"Tell me about it."

"About my day?" – I looked confused.

"Yes. I meant what I said today. I would like to get to know you if you'll let me."

I told him about the restaurant and our somehow weird combination with Nate to work together, be divorced and be part a of each other's life. Then I somehow shifted to the topic of Brian moving in with Lara and me.

"You probably have a man knocking on your door every day. How come you are single then?" – he asked

"What makes you so sure I am single?"

"You are talking to me while having a bath naked, and who knows what you are doing. If you are in a relationship, I can't imagine letting you have a bath alone." – I laughed and realized I had totally forgotten about how to speak to a man or how to flirt. My main speaking partner was Lara, who did not always respond.

"I am bad at this. Sorry. My main focus has been Lara the past seven years."

"Not as bad as my driving. Would you like to have dinner with me?"

"Yeah, sure." – I bit my lip, and we decided to go out on the weekend when both of us are free from kids.

When we hung up, I looked around the bath and realized how right he was. When was the last time I was with somebody? When was the last time somebody shared a bath with me, or even a romantic meal? I glanced at my legs; it said it all. Having the perfect shaved legs were not my priority. My lady friend was abandoned, and it was time for me to get out there. I let the water out from the bath and booked a waxing appointment, manicure, and pedicure for the next morning. It was time to have a day for myself. I texted Nate that I would not be going to work tomorrow. I wasn't looking for my next prince charming, but someone to take care of me for a change. Pay for a nice dinner or cook me something. Do something which was more for adults and not only watch cartoons. When I went to sleep, I had a smile on my face and thought of the exciting date coming up.

The next day, when I woke up, I wanted to text Brian to ask if he had a move-in date already and before I got the chance, he wrote to me.

Hey! Got my move-out date. Saturday morning, they will come and take everything out. I will be at your or our place in the evening. We can have a drink in the evening as a celebration.

Shit. It was the same day. I wanted to help Brian, but it was the first date I'd had in a while. I decided to reply later. I took Lara to school, but this time through the drop-off. Before she could leave, Ramos was knocking on my window, which scared me for a second. I pulled the window down with a smile.

"Why in such a hurry?" – he asked

"Have a lot of appointments today. I am sorry you can't scratch my car today."

"Funny. Alright. Can't wait to see you on Saturday. Dress nice, but comfortable."

"Comfortable?" – I looked at him confused, but before he could respond, the cars behind me started to honk.

I drove off to my appointments. First, I started with a pedicure, then a manicure and at the end with waxing. I forgot how painful it was. I was screaming and asked them to stop several times for a quick break. I remembered the reason I started shaving. Women are crazy to do so many things for beauty. When I finished, I realized I had to do this for myself after all this suffering. If I back out now, I will only regret it.

Guess what? Have my first date on Saturday with a hot dad from school. I'll leave your keys in the restaurant, and we can do something Sunday as a welcome.

Sent. I put my phone away and drove home to do some cleaning. Before that, I called Steve to drop by for a coffee. As his business was booming, he spent more time home with Nicole and the kids. Nicole was out grocery shopping. Steve was working while watching with his other eye how Vincent and Jessie were playing.

Vincent was the firstborn and the first baby in the family. I remember we wanted to be there almost every day to just hold him. Get our noses full of baby smell, touch his soft little body and kiss his cute little toes. He was so peaceful and cute. Brown eyes like his mother and dark black hair. He was a year older than Lara, and they loved playing together. When Jessie was born, who was the loudest little angel on earth, she joined them in the playing parties. The three of them were more like brothers and sisters than cousins. Steve and I always wanted to have kids who get along as well as we did. Until now, we did a good job. I sat down with the kids to play while talking with Steve about work and my new date.

"What did Nate say to your idea?" – he asked while closing the laptop and turning towards us.

"He has nothing to say. We are happily divorced, and Lara seemed happy when she saw Brian on the couch the other morning. I think she can handle it."

"What did you just say?" – he stood up and walked over to sit next to us

"That Lara can handle it."

"No. Not that. What was Brian doing on your couch?"

"Oh, that…" – I paused and stood up to start going. It was time to avoid the conversation which was coming up. – "He came over, and we fell asleep while drinking, then Lara came home with Nate. But I will go slowly, have to run to pick up Lara."

He stood up to kiss me goodbye while I was trying to avoid eye contact. I kissed Vincent and Jessie a few times and made my way towards the exit.

"What are you not telling me, Tess?"

"He is moving into the guest bedroom."

"Nate?" – he opened his eyes wide and raised his voice

"No. Hell no. Brian."

"What? Why?" – his voice got louder and louder.

"He has some problems with the roof and has to completely move out, and I offered until it's done." – Steve looked down and shook his head. - "Don't be judgy. I know what I am doing. He is just a friend in need."

"Yeah, sure. Just don't be stupid, alright? For Lara's sake."

I kissed him on the cheek and hugged him tight, and left. I was still thinking about why he and mom were always against Brian. I know he hurt me a few times - alright, a lot of times, but he was also there for me. I had a date in front of me, and I should focus on that.

Saturday was a busy day, with dropping off keys for Brian at the restaurant, then taking Lara to Nate's place, listening to him giving me a lesson about my decisions and then getting ready for the date.

Ramos said I should dress comfortably. What did that even mean? I was standing in front of the clothes and realized I had no idea what he meant. I texted Sarah for her advice.

If someone says a comfortable dress code, what would you wear?

Not even a minute passed, and my phone was ringing. It was Sarah.

"Hi Sarah"

"Who is he? Tell me everything?" – her voice was full of enthusiasm

"Nobody…at least yet. Help me with clothes. The rest I will tell you tomorrow."

"Well, for you, high heels are also comfortable, so it's not really specific. Did he say anything else which might give you a hint?

"Just some tapas place he likes, which reminds him of home."

"You are going to Little Spain. I got the perfect outfit. Wear a dress, something which is not tight, and you can move, and flat shoes with a small bag." – I stopped and wondered how she knew what we were doing.

"What is little Spain? How did you guess so fast?"

"It's like little Venice, but little Spain. It's the best area in the city to remind you of the Latino culture. It must be there. They have the best Tapas place I have ever been to, and also there is a famous salsa club next to it. That's the flat shoes part." – I could hear in her voice she was smiling and getting happier than I was for the night ahead.

"Thanks, expert. I'll let you know what it was at the end."

I took a shower first, then curled my hair a bit, put on some light makeup, and a nice light red lipstick. I chose the red dress, which had short sleeves and an A-shape. The end of the dress had a little bit of lace, which gave that additional sexy touch. It was one of the most comfortable dresses I had as it was nothing tight on it, and I could breathe normally after dinner. I put on black ballerinas, which matched the small bag I chose to go with it. I stopped in front of the mirror, and I saw a young Tess going out again. I felt young and free. It was a great feeling to see the adult me taking the next step in life to get a new partner and going out again on dates. Ramos might not be the perfect match for me, but you never know what the night might bring.

The doorbell rang and I went out. I didn't want to invite him up on the first date, but rather show him where I live later if it goes somewhere. As I started to walk down the stairs, I wrote Brian a message.

I hope everything was alright with the keys. Get settled, and tomorrow we can celebrate. Can't wait roomy. See you later.

When I opened the main entrance, Ramos was standing there in beige chino pants and a white t-shit. He came towards me and kissed me on the cheek.

"You look very nice. I think you got the perfect understanding of the dress code." – he said while checking me out from head to toe.

"Are you going to tell me where we are going?"

He unlocked his car and showed me the way with his hands.

"No, I think you have to wait, but I am sure you will like it." – he opened the door for me.

We didn't talk much during the car ride, it was more about choosing the right music, and I was looking out the window where we are going. It was my first date since

Nate, and I had a feeling it was a first for him in a long time too.

"I am sorry, I didn't do this kind of a thing for a long time." – I spilled it.

"You mean drive with a handsome man in a car to an unknown place?"

"I got divorced when Lara was 1 year old, since then she has been the center of my attention, so I haven't had the time to go out to be with adults at all, except with family and some friends."

"I understand. It is new to me too, but we will get hold of it once our stomach is full with some good tapas." – he stopped the car and pointed to the right side to the tapas place Sarah mentioned. "We are here."

When we got out, he shook hands with the waiters as well as with some guests. For a brief second, I thought of my first date with Nate when he took me to his restaurant. The tapas place was very cozy with only a few tables. The walls were red, and the whole place was full of decorations from bulls and pictures of the "La Tomatina". The waiters had some Spanish custom clothing with a small sombrero. I suddenly felt like jumping to Spain in a small street in

Madrid. The waiter showed us a round table in the middle of the restaurant where a red rose was placed on one plate. Ramos pulled the chair out for me. I took the rose in my hand and smelled it. It was fresh and smelled beautiful.

"Thank you. This is very kind." – I placed the rose to the side and turned back to Ramos – "Are you an owner here, or you bring all your dates here?" – I picked up his eye contact and didn't let him look any other way.

"It is my ex-wife's family restaurant. I come here only with Jake as a date. We love the couple Tapas, which I also pre-ordered for us, if you don't mind. It is a great combination of the best offers they have." – He changed the subject so nicely, I didn't even notice.

"Is it with meat?" – I asked

"Are you a vegetarian? You don't look like one." – I opened my eyes widely and wondered if he just told me that I am fat.

"I am not, but why did you say I don't look like one?" – I crossed my arms and took my warrior position.

"Most girls who are vegetarian, vegan or whatever come in and take the menu and start listing everything they don't like before even ordering. You look at the bulls on the walls with a sparkle in your eye. Vegetarians wouldn't do that." – I smiled and put my arms back to my lap. He knew just what to say.

"Thank you! I actually own a restaurant, and I love to see other places. The bulls and the decoration are really fascinating."

"I love it as well. What kind of place do you have?" – he bent towards me and didn't take his eyes of me while I gave him an introduction of my business, how it started and how I got there. To me, it was amazing to see how somebody could pay so much attention, and his eyes were just looking at me. It was hard to know what he was thinking, if the story was interesting or not, but I was sure that I liked the way he looked at me.

My story was broken in half when my phone rang. It was Brian. I didn't pick up, but he rang again and again.

"You can pick up. Maybe it's an emergency." – he said while taking a sip of his wine.

"I am sorry. It will be short" – I picked up the phone and turned a bit to the side. "Hey. Everything alright?"

"Yeah. I forgot about your date. Sorry. Just wanted to let you know I moved in, but I lost my key somehow on the street, so I can't get out." – I closed my eyes and thought the date is over. – "Tess?"

"I can come home and give you mine if you need to get out." - I added

"Don't even think about it. I am fine, just if you see it before the entrance when you come home, pick it up. I don't want you here. Enjoy your date and have fun. You deserve it."

"Thanks, Brian" – I smiled and looked at Ramos, who was surprised to hear another man's voice.

"Maybe we can have breakfast all together in the morning." – he laughed in the background.

"Bye, Brian." – I hung up and turned back to Ramos. – "Sorry. A friend who just moved in with me lost my apartment key."

"Do you need to get back? We can drive and come back if you want."

"No. No. He is fine. Sorry." – Just the best timing ever, the waiter came with the food and placed everything in the middle. There was so much food that you could feed an army. I was used to small portions and more courses, but this all looked just amazing. There was Calamari, Chopito, several types of olives, chorizo, Empanadas, fried cheese, Prawns made in different styles, potatoes, cheese and some spreads too.

"I like that you are so foody." – Ramos smiled and followed me in the eating process.

"It all tastes so good. It's amazing." – I closed my eyes with every bite and enjoyed the flavors that burst in my mouth. Ramos looked at me and laughed at me how much I enjoyed every bite.

"I have never seen somebody enjoy food this much. You are something, Tess." – he paused and looked down at his plate. – "So how come this friend is moving in with you? Are you a thing, or is it more complicated?"

I knew the questions would come, but I was ready for that. Nate already asked me the same, and I could just repeat the same answer.

"We are just friends. His apartment had a flood, and I offered him to stay in the spare room. He is also the godfather of Lara, so they get along very well. He should be out in 2 weeks."

"Oh. That's very nice of you. I hope you will be so

generous the next time I have a flood as well."

"Of course. This is what somebody does when you work in hospitality your whole life. My door is always open." - we laughed, and then it was my time to ask his story. – "So now you know my story. What is yours?"

"I am divorced, as you already know. My wife left me when Jake was born. She was not ready to be a mother, so she packed her stuff and disappeared. We often come to this tapas place with Jake because he hopes she will be here one day, but she wasn't. He grew up with the hope of having a mother. My ex-wife's family is supporting us, and they don't know anything about her as well. She is just gone. The grandparents helped me with Jake when he was a baby. I didn't even know how to hold a diaper, feed or play with him. When Jake turned one, I started my own company. I realized in that year that there are books about babies only for mothers, but for single dads, none. So I made an App called – Daddy is Here. It basically shows you daily what and when to do it. From feeding to walking and some good advice on how to get your kid to sleep longer. The App had such a huge success that I didn't work more than 2 hours a day after three years. It was bought by one of the bigger companies and I was left as CEO. We are developing more and more and focusing on older children now, but it means more time with Jake for me. This is why I can bring him to school, pick him up, be part of parent clubs and have dates with beautiful moms."

His story was very touching as well as inspiring. Instead of bringing him down and losing faith, he used everything he learned from his baby to make a great business. We often think parents teach the children, but his story is proof that it is often the other way around.

We shared during the meal some funny parenting stories of our children. The conversation just had a natural flow. It was so different after the car ride. I really thought we will have a bad night, but this is really good. When we finished the bottle of wine, Ramos ordered a bottle of water for take away and the bill without even asking for something else. I looked confused, and he saw it, but instead of getting worried, he took my hand and held it while responding to my face.

"Don't worry. The night is young. I have planned something else for which we need to get going. Shall we?"

"Let me go to the toilet, and we can go." – when I stood up, I turned back for an additional question – "Why the water if we are leaving?"

He made a charming smile and replied.

"To keep you hydrated."

Well, that just confused me even more. I texted Sarah from the toilet that she was right about the place and that we are going somewhere else. Maybe for that place, I needed the casual part of the dress code. I re-applied my lipstick and was ready to go.

When I got back, Ramos was already at the exit speaking with the waiter and laughing. When I got there, he opened the door for me. The kind older waiter made a kind smile and waved goodbye to us.

"Where are we going now?" – I placed my hand under his arm and held him.

"Have you danced before?"

"When I was younger. I did Jazz Ballet mostly, but I like all kinds of dance types. Why?" – I turned to him, and he just pointed towards the place in front of us.

It was a dark little entrance to a club. There were people in front with cigarettes in their hands, but no music. We exchanged a look and walked across the street to enter this small place. Ramos opened one door, and then I heard a little bit of music, but then we went down to the basement where the Latino music was getting louder and louder. When we went through the last door, it was all clear. We are at a Salsa Bar. They were playing Romeo Santos, who had a lot of songs where you can dance Bachata, Salsa or Merengue. I took each step slower and slower as I started to gaze over the dance floor. There wasn't a single person standing on the side or at the bar. Everybody was dancing. It was mostly couples. The single people were dancing in groups, but the dance floor was full. Most of them had such a good feeling for music. They felt the rhythm and their bodies were moving the same way. It was like we jumped into a Dirty Dancing movie.

"Wanna dance?" – Ramos held his hand out. I nodded as I was still in shock from the dancers. He took my bag and the water and placed them behind the bar into a safety box. He took me by the hand and moved me to the dance floor.

"Just lose yourself and move with me." – he picked up my chin to looked me in the eyes. He placed one hand on my back the other one held my hand. – "We are going two steps to your right, then two steps left, and then we turn. Basic Bachata"

"Alright, Patrick Swayze."

When the music slowed, he moved me closer to him, and we made small steps in the same place, but moving around and around. He pushed me closer to him, and our bodies touched. With only looking at his eyes, I knew if we were going left or right. When the music was faster, we moved to the rhythm. Our hips were moving together, and it felt like being part of the great dancers on the dance floor. When the music changed, another guy came to me and asked me for a dance. I didn't even have time to respond, and Ramos was also changing a partner. It felt a bit weird, but with each partner, the style of dance was different. I changed with several men and then I needed a break and went to the side to take the water.

"Are you alright?" – Ramos stood in front of me.

"I needed some water. This place is amazing. I really love it."

"Come dance with me." – he pulled me with him back to the dance floor.

He didn't say any instruction or anything, we just felt the music, and we moved. It was an amazing experience. One I have never felt in my life. I felt so free and relaxed.

After a few hours of dancing, it was already 2 am. I felt the time to go home. My legs were already very tired, and I felt too sweaty.

"I'll take you home." – Ramos said, and we walked back to his car. On the way there, I was just talking about the dance and how amazing the night was. He laughed at me several times and followed my hands as I was trying to explain something. In the car, we continued listening to Romeo Santos, and I pretended to dance while Ramos was making a video or picture of me every time we stopped at a traffic light.

When we got back to my place, I stopped in front of the entrance door to find first my apartment keys, which Brian lost.

"Your keys?" – he said

"I didn't think I would find them. Must be my lucky day." – I turned to open the door, but then I stopped and turned back to see Ramos leaning back to his car. – "Would you like to come up?" – I opened the door and went inside.

"I should be going. You have other guests upstairs" – he smiled and walked over to me.

"Thank you for the lovely evening." – with that, he took

my hand and pulled me close to him, and kissed me. Our bodies touched the same way when we were on the dance floor. His lips were warm and wet. With every kiss, I felt goosebumps all over my body. I wanted him to kiss me the whole evening, but it was worth the wait. It was an unforgettable kiss. He then moved back, stopped and said – "Good night, Tess."

CHAPTER 3

I don't remember the last time I woke up with such a grin on my face. My feet were still in the Latino bar and moving to the rhythm in my head. When I got out of bed, I continued dancing into the bathroom to wash my face. The last time I really looked at myself was the night I signed my divorce papers, and I went out to celebrate with friends. That night, I came home and stared in the mirror, thinking if it was the right decision to break the family for my unhappiness. Was it really such a big thing to be cheated to leave Nate? Couldn't we have worked it out somehow? Will my decision have an influence on Lara and the person she turns out to be? I criticized myself like never before. This time it was different. I didn't think about it as a bad thing, but rather something which will bring back a little flame and chemistry into my life. I couldn't decide if Ramos was the person I wanted to wake up to every day, but he was definitely on the top of the list. He was very charming, an incredibly good dancer, and his life story about his work was so inspiring. I really thought he would be a good example for Lara as well. Maybe I shouldn't move that fast in my head and take a few steps back to see how the whole thing is going, but until now, it was good. Not having Lara in the morning always made my morning ritual slower. Normal breakfast, Coffee and catching up on work, and sometimes even watching an episode of series with breakfast. I changed my PJ's to a bra and nice underpants and walked out of the bedroom to get breakfast. I loved to walk around half-naked, listen to music, and get dressed slowly when Lara is not around.

"Alexa, play coffeeshop music" – I instructed Alexa, who was my main chatting partner in the kitchen. I started slowly dancing to the open fridge and thinking about what I should have for breakfast.

"Is your performance part of everyday breakfast, cause I am definitely getting up earlier then." - said Brian from the guestroom entrance. He had his cheeky smile, and even in the morning, he was ready for a good joke.

"Shit. I forgot you are here." – I closed the fridge and went to the bathroom to take my bathrobe. I slapped my face a few times on the way. How could I forget he was here? I am insane to walk around like this. I wrote a post-it on the bedside table with "Brian lives here" to remind myself should I be in the mood to walk half-naked again.

"Sorry for that. I forgot you are here. Breakfast?" – I opened the fridge again and couldn't look him in the eyes.

"Eggs? I'll help you. How was the date? You seem very happy." – he said while coming over and starting the kettle to make tea and coffee.

"I'll make you a great omelet, which Nate thought me. Can you make us a coffee? - I took out the ingredients and started cooking while telling Brian all about the date. He didn't question much, only smiled and prepared to ask me if we had sex, but I didn't let him speak to avoid that part of the conversation. – "It was really a good evening. I hope I will see him again, outside of parent's meetings. Did you settle in? I found your keys in front of the entrance. Try not losing them next time, otherwise, you're sleeping on the terrace." – I smiled and handed him his breakfast.

"Wow. This looks amazing. At least something good from Nate. Oh, and yeah. All went well. I have everything out in the room. I will go shopping today for some food and things I need for training, but otherwise all good. If you need anything from the store, tell me, and I can get it."

"Great. Mostly stuff for Lara. I'll text you a list."

"Please don't tell me to buy tampons. I am not ready for that yet." – I laughed and shook my head. It was clear he has no idea about women nor children.

We enjoyed our breakfast together, and then I got a call to go into work, so I had to run off, but we planned to do something just the two of us once Lara was with Nate again.

The whole week passed in a blink of an eye. I hadn't heard from Ramos, neither did I see him in school. Jake was apparently sick, and both of them were at home. Lara was quite down without him in school. After two weeks since our last date, Ramos finally called. To make him feel bad, I didn't pick up and left my phone in the restaurant office. I went to the parent meeting without it and thought he could wait. As usual, Joanna was the first person to arrive.

"Hey, how is everything?" – she hugged me and handed me a paper with tasks, which I quickly glanced through.

"Hey. How come I am always with Ramos? I haven't even seen him for weeks."

"Well. He requested to be with you. Poor Jake had chicken pocks, and he got it as well. They were both quite bad, but he is coming today. Didn't he call you?" – Joanna said. Now, I felt bad about myself. Just as my subconscious got to me, Ramos walked in with a smile on his face like he was on full energy.

"Hello, ladies. Tess can I speak to you?" – we moved to the side, but I saw Joanna following us with her eyes.

"I am so sorry I ignored you. I didn't know about the sickness." – I placed a hand on his arm, which was for showing support, but instead, I felt strong muscles and strength.

"Hey. Don't worry. I am feeling bad not telling you about it, but I wanted to keep you healthy. Are you available Friday for a night out dancing again?" – my smile came back, and I just nodded.

Throughout the whole meeting, Ramos and I shared looks and smiles with each other. In some way, I was half undressing him with my eyes, but that was just the hormones speaking and the time I'd spent alone. After the meeting, I waved Ramos goodbye and wanted to go the other way, but before I could, the two single women, Jackie and Julie, stopped me.

"So…the two of you… is it something?" – Julie asked with a judgmental look.

"We are just hanging out."

"You don't seem like it's just hanging out. Are you sure? Cause he is a real catch, and I would definitely have a taste of that Latino." – Added Jackie while licking her lips.

"No. I am sure. If you'll excuse me, I have to go to pick up Lara. Great talking to you." – I walked between them and turned my eyes. I hated those kinds of girls in school and at work.

Lara and I were going towards the car when I saw Jackie all over Ramos. They were just talking, but she touched him at least three times. I tried to pay attention to Lara's story, but it was still annoying me. Thankfully, I had black sunglasses, and my eyes were not visible, but I was staring at them. When we got into the car, I took my phone out and started texting.

Something came up. Have to cancel Friday. Maybe you can go with somebody else if you are still free. Xx Tess

Sent. I was not jealous, more angry. I had no time nor the energy to play games. I was over it and didn't want to be part of some handsome man's game. I turned to Lara in the backseat and saw her cute smile looking at me.

"What do you say we have a fun cartoon evening with

Uncle Brian on Friday?"

"Yes! We can watch Frozen 1 and 2 with popcorn, and you can make that good cheese sauce. Brian would love that."

"I think he wouldn't like the movie, but you'll have to ask him. I am sure you can convince him."

We drove home, where we got back to the smell of a fresh meal. It was Brian creating his masterpiece in the kitchen.

"Welcome home. I made you a meal and thought we could finally hang out Friday. What do you say, princess?" – He kissed Lara on the top of her head and bent down to hear a response.

"Mommy and I said the same. Would you watch Frozen 1 and 2 with us? Mommy will make her special cheese sauce." – Lara said while making her puppy eyes and staring into Brians's soul, who, of course, couldn't say no.

"Mommy will also buy wine for Mommy and Brian to make the movie even better." – I winked at Brian and walked away, leaving them and getting the school bag to Lara's room and my things to the living room. When I took my phone out, I saw 2 missed calls from Ramos and a few messages.

Somebody is you. I don't want to go without you.

Can I help somehow? Everything alright?

Call me if you want to speak.

Of course, he didn't know I saw him with Jackie, but I also didn't want to be played. I was not calling for sure. I tried to write a neutral message.

Just promised Brian to hang out with him and Lara. Movie night. Next time.

Up to Friday, I had several calls and messages from Ramos, but I didn't respond. I wanted to leave it cool down. Friday, when I waited for Lara in front of the school, Jackie parked just in front of me and to my surprise, she was not alone. Ramos got out too. I caught Jackies' eyes on me, who raised her eyebrow and turned to Ramos and touched him on the face. She turned to look at me, I just turned and got out of the car. What a bitch. Ramos saw her look and moved his face away from her hand, and got out of the car to ran after me.

"Tess. Wait." – he took me by the hand and stopped me.

"Sorry, Ramos. I am not one for games. I have to pick up Lara." – I shook his hand away and continued walking, but he came after me.

"You are misunderstanding. My car broke down two days ago. I called you several times, but you never picked up, and she offered to help out." – Again, me with my bad judgments, but no.

"She almost kissed you in the car. Listen, Ramos, I like you a lot, but I can't be part of the game. Nate cheated on me, and it broke me into pieces." – My eyes were filling with tears, but I swallowed and didn't let them out.

"I like you, Tess. I am sorry. You have to trust me." – he picked up my head by the chin and cupped my face. We just looked at each other, and then he kissed me. For a second, I forgot we are at school surrounding by people. People who loved to talk. I knew that Nate would hear it from somebody else. I invited Ramos and Jake to join us on Friday for movies and popcorn. I would leave it as a surprise for Lara and Brian. I called Nate to tell him.

"Hey. Are you free?"

"There are a lot of guests here, but all good. What's up?" – he responded, but I could hear in his voice he is in the middle of cooking and sounded distracted.

"I met this guy and wanted to let you know…."

"Tess. I accepted Brian moving in. It's alright, just don't mix pleasure with family. Don't get Lara involved early. She is too emotional, and it's not healthy to get her upset and see you sleeping around."

"Nate, you just talked to me like I am a whore. You broke me, and I can't trust anyone. I just told you this because I am going for something serious…" – tears ran down my cheeks – "I wanted to let you know before you hear it from some other parents."

"Parents?"

"Bye, Nate." – I hung up.

Once again, I thought about his feelings, but all I got was a slap in the face. How could he think I am sleeping around when our child is with me 99% of the time? When would I have the time for that?

At home, we prepared everything for the movie night. PJ's on, a lot of popcorn, nachos and my special cheese sauce, which was basically two types of cheddar cheese melted with some pepper. Brian put all the shutters down and lit up candles everywhere to make it cozier. We had a lot of pillows on the sofa and of course at least two bottles of wine. I loved cartoons since I was a child, but Brian always made fun of me. He was ready for a long night of pain .

"I have a little surprise for the two of you. I hope you don't mind." – I said when Lara and Brian turned to me with a surprised face.

"Jake is here?" – Lara added.

"How do you know everything?" – I smiled and wondered how she could know me that well.

"I saw you and Jake's dad in school." – oh crap. I forgot she might see that.

"Saw what?" – Brian added.

Lara took a Barbie and Ken and showed how they kiss. Brian and I just laughed. The doorbell rang, and they were just on time to join us. Brian stood up and walked to the door to greet them with me. As well, he wanted to check out Ramos.

Jake ran up the stairs with his PJ's, and with a smile and wave, ran into the apartment and hugged Lara like they hadn't seen each other for days. Ramos was behind with a bag in his hand and the other one behind his back.

"I am sorry. Jake was happier to see Lara tonight than to hang out with me." – he was a bit out of breath when he got up. He had a onesie on, which I found very entertaining, and it was in the shape of Whiney the Pooh, while Jake was the little piglet. I thought it was adorable.

"Nice outfit, mate. I am Brian. Nice to meet you." – They shook hands, and Ramos bent over to kiss me on the cheek. He then pulled out a nice bouquet of roses behind his back and gave it to me.

"Wow. Thanks. Come in" – I took the bouquet from him. Brian and I exchanged a look, and he showed me a thumbs up with a big smile. I smelled the roses and walked over to the kitchen to put them in a vase.

"This is a beautiful flat. No wonder you moved in." – Ramos said, turning to Brian.

"Yeah. Tess is an angel to let me stay."

"Hey. I thought I am your angel," – Lara added from the back with an angry look on her face.

"You are, princess. Come, let's start that movie of yours." – Brian showed the way to the sofa and came to the kitchen to open the wines.

"He is nice." – Brian said and looked at me.

"Wine?" – I shouted to Ramos.

"I am driving. Thank you" – before I could reply to that, Brian was faster.

"It's a sleepover. Didn't you get the full memo?"

I could only hear laughter and no response. I hit Brian in the arm.

"Are you crazy? The kids are here." – I hit Brian again.

"Even better. They are distracted." – he poured the wine and walked away with a proud smile.

The evening was really fun. The kids sat on pillows on the floor and commented on everything while the three of us were on the sofa. We talked quietly. Brian and Ramos were getting along very well. Brian even told some stories about me, like when he brought me home from graduation and my whole back was out of the coat, and every person saw my underwear. We drank around four bottles at the end.

Jake and Lara looked sleepy, and they fell asleep on the floor holding each other's hands. We all took a photo of them before moving them.

"I hate waking them up." – Ramos said.

"Then don't" – I turned to him.

Brian stood up and left the two of us while starting to clean up.

"You can stay. Both of you. Lara has an extra bed in her room, and you… well…you can sleep with Brian or on the couch." - I teased. He placed his hand on my neck and pulled me in for a kiss. – "I take this as a yes to my offer." – he nodded.

I stood up and went to Lara's room to prepare everything for Jake. When I was ready, I went over to wake them up and move them. Ramos took Jake under his arm and moved him over without waking him up. Lara was already too heavy for me to take her, but Brian was here. He came over, and without even asking him, he picked her up, kissed her on the head and brought her to her room.

I went to the bathroom to take a shower. I took out an old lingerie piece that I wore the last time I wanted to make love to Nate. It was a nice black dress with delicate eyelash lace. I took my bathrobe over it, before Brian saw more than he should, again. As I was about to exit, I heard my name a few times between Brian and Ramos. I wasn't sure what they said, as before I could eavesdrop, they heard my steps and stopped speaking.

"Alright, I am leaving you young people. Have fun. Good night. See you tomorrow." – Brian smiled at me, waved to Ramos and left the room.

Ramos walked towards me and kissed me on the lips. I pulled away from him and asked.

"What were you talking about? I heard my name?"

"Just boy stuff. No worries. Can I have a shower? This PJ is super warm, and I can't wait to get it off."

"I can help you with that." – I put on a flirty look and started to unzip the onesie from the front, but he took my hand and stopped me.

"Shower first." – he kissed me on the cheek and went to the bathroom.

I took off the bathrobe and placed it on the chair beside the bed. I took out my phone to check my emails. First, I saw several phone calls from Nate, then from other numbers and loads of Emails. Before I called Nate, I saw he'd also sent me several messages.

Tess!! Pick up!!! It's urgent!!

Where are you?

Tess!! It's not a joke…. The restaurant had a fire.

I jumped up, already getting ready to changed. My heart started to beat even faster. I felt my blood pressure getting higher and higher. I couldn't lose that place. I continued reading his last message sent a few minutes ago.

We will talk tomorrow… what was wrong with you? YOU HAVE TO BE AVAILABLE. It is all handled. Just a few stoves need to be changed. No other problem. We solved it with the team. Ordered the new ones, which will be delivered tomorrow. We have a full staff meeting tomorrow. BE THERE!!!!

Thank God it was alright, and Nate was there. I can't believe that I missed it and left my phone just like that.

"Are you alright?" – Ramos said, standing at the doorway with a towel around his waist. I looked up, and my anger changed in a second at the sight of him. His body was still a bit wet. A few drops on water on his breast and perfectly shaped stomach. His upper body was like a young Brad Pitt with a touch of Latino. His skin was smooth, and there was no single hair on his chest or stomach. Probably waxed to emphasize his muscles. I placed my phone on the nightstand, walked over while his eyes were scanning my lingerie up and down. I held his neck with one hand, and the other I placed on his muscular chest. He moved down and picked me up by my thighs while I held him by the neck. Our lips didn't leave each other for a second. His lips were wet, and his tongue danced with mine. We stood there for a second; his hands held my thighs strongly, holding me solid close to his pelvis. He moved closer to the bed, where he bent down and placed me slowly on my back. Our lips separated to catch some air. He took off his towel, and I glanced down at his gift. We shared a smile, and our lips were back, sharing a passionate long-lasting kiss. Both of us felt an enormous hunger for each other.

The next day I woke up with a smile on my face. I stopped the alarm and rolled over to see Ramos staring at me already.

"Good morning, Guapa." – he said and gave a kiss on my forehead.

"Coffee and Breakfast?" – I got up and turned towards him.

"Can I have you instead of both?" – I laughed and got up to get myself presentable for the kids and Brian.

Ramos had his eyes all over me and followed me in the bathroom for a shower. While washing my face, I took a few glances at him.

"I will ask Brian to give you some clothes instead of the outfit. I'll be right back." – I went out of the room to see Brian sitting in the kitchen with already coffee prepared and making breakfast for Lara and Jake, who were also up.

"Why are you up so early?" – I hugged and kissed Lara, then Jake.

"We were excited to go to the park. Can we, mommy?" – Lara looked at me with her puppy eyes.

"Sorry sweety, I have to go to the restaurant. Maybe Ramos can take you both." - I went over to Brian and whispered to him quietly. – "There was a fire in the restaurant. I have to go soon."

"Do you need some help? Was anybody hurt?" – Brian worriedly.

"Everybody is good. I'll see when I get there what should be done. Thanks. Oh…" – I paused and blushed. – "Can you lend Ramos some clothes?"

"I need more information before that." – he got back his

cheeky smile.

"Later."

Brian went to the room to pick up some clothes and handed them over to me, which I took to Ramos, waiting naked. I wanted to have another round with him once I saw him, but I tried to behave and only touched his chest and gave him a kiss.

"Can you maybe take the kids to the park now? I have to run to the restaurant."

"Of course. Let me know if you need some help. I'll make them lunch and bring Lara back in the afternoon." – he agreed and got dressed.

"Can you bring her to the restaurant? I might be staying longer. I can then show you around."

He nodded, and we went out to the kitchen. Lara and Jake were ready to leave, so we hurried up and went all out to our separate ways.

I ran to the restaurant as fast as possible, only stopping for some takeaway breakfast for all the employees coming in extra early for the meeting. I was the first one to be there, so I packed out the food in the training kitchen, checked the fire and the issues we had to fix. Nate was the next to be in who had dark eye circles and looked tired.

"Sorry for not picking up. We were watching a movie. I didn't hear the phone." – I started to excuse myself and handed over a coffee to him.

"No problem. Thankfully nobody got hurt."

The rest of the staff came in soon after and were happy to see the breakfast prepared.

"Thank you all for coming in. Please dig in and eat and drink as much as you want. I know most of you had a long night with the fire and cleaning up. I am very sorry that I wasn't here to help you. I am glad to hear that nobody was hurt, and we all knew how to handle the situation before it got worse. We ordered the new parts, which will be delivered next week. Until then, we will need to work in the training kitchen. I know it's smaller and slower, but we have to make it work for a few days." – I said, while everybody nodded and smiled at me.

"Please prepare as much as possible in advance; we will take off the food from this week's menu, which is harder to make here." – Nate added.

Nate and I joined the team in eating, and we talked about

nicer things a bit and how and what to change on the menu. After an hour, the team left, and Nate and I stayed behind to get the insurance and order sorted out.

"So, what did you really do yesterday? You always have your phone with you." – Nate asked. I knew the question will come sooner or later.

"We watched Frozen 1 and 2." – I responded while starting to pack the kitchen to move to the training area.

"We?"

"Brian, Lara, Jake and his dad. We had a bit more to drink, and my phone was in the kitchen."

"So that's the one you kissed in the school?" – he laughed and started to help me pack.

"Yeah. I am not happy about it, but I like him."

"Just remember what we discussed."

"I know Nate. Remember? Lara grew up with me mostly. I gave up everything for her. It is nice that somebody takes care of me for a change." – I looked sadly at him.

"I am sorry to be so mean with you and always disagree. You deserve it, and I know how hard it is to be alone. I hope you will find somebody to make you happy. I promise to change and even help you," - Before he could continue, the rest of the staff came in, and the cooking and preparations started.

The day was very chaotic, and I wasn't paying attention to the time. One of the waitresses came to the office and told me Lara was here with somebody. I forgot about Ramos. I jumped up, and before I could get out, Nate followed and Lara jumped on him while screaming "Daddy".

"Hi guys." – I said and smiled at Ramos, who bent and gave me a kiss on the cheek. – "This is Nate, my ex-husband and best Chef in town. Ramos, Jake's dad."

Nate and Ramos shook hands, and the kids followed Nate to the playground.

"Let me show you around." – I said to Ramos, and we went around the restaurant starting from the terrace. Ramos loved the place. He was comparing it to the Tapas place we went to, and it was a whole other level. He had never been in a Michelin Star restaurant before. We said we would come here for a date one night after the fire issues were sorted. We stayed there a few hours, and then Ramos went home with Jake, and I drove home with Lara.

At home, Brian was sitting on the sofa, looking totally depressed. Lara came over to him, gave him a hug and went to her room. She was a very emotional child and loved to give kisses and hugs to everybody. I didn't know if she knew if something was wrong or not, but she knew what to say and what to do.

Without saying anything, I took out a red wine with two glasses. Poured into both and sat next to Brian, handing him one over.

"Tell me." – he looked up and took the glass.

"I invested so much in that crazy apartment. They called me and said they will have to destroy it and rebuild it. It will take months to get it ready or even more. I am not sure what to do."

"You can stay here, of course, but don't you think it is better to sell and buy something else?"

"I will have to check, but it will take months. It might be better to buy something new, but I don't want to be on your back with living here." – I placed my hand on his and smiled.

"Lara loves you, and I like to drink with somebody. Don't worry about us." – Brian looked at me and smiled with a bit of relief.

"So how was he?" – he teased

"Well…." - I bit my lip and paused. – "It was great. He knew his way around, and I really enjoyed it." – I put on a huge smile.

"The second will be even better. I hope he will make you happy." – to not let him tease me all the time, I added.

"You mean third."

CHAPTER 4

We celebrated the second year of the three of us living together. Brian decided to sell his old house and start a new dream house from scratch. It took instead of months, years to finish. Lara loved having him there. He never brought girls home when she was around and behaved like an adult most of the time. I enjoyed having his company and also was glad to have him support me on my dates. Instead of Sarah, he came into the bedroom and helped me choose something. He always wanted to have something sexy, but it was not really my style. We had our last night together in a week, and Lara and I prepared a surprise farewell party and gift for him.

Since Nate and I divorced, Ramos was my first relationship. We had been together almost two years and decided not to move in until the children were ready. Jake and Lara had ups and downs as they grew, but in the end, they always found their way back. Holiday celebrations were the nicest because we did them all together. Mom and her husband were over for one day at Christmas and Steve and his family on another. We played games with the kids and had a lot of fun. On those days, I forgot about all the problems in the World. Ramos and I decided to have date nights every week where it is only the two of us to get to know each other better. Until we had fun, Jake and Lara were usually watching movies with Brian. After so many cartoons, he even started to like them. Jackie and Julie from the committee were not very happy about the relationship and were doing their best to make me jealous, but it didn't work. I trusted Ramos.

For Brian's farewell, Ramos and Jake were responsible for the food they organized from the famous Tapas Restaurant. We decorated the flat with balloons and a board with farewell wishes. As a farewell gift, Lara and I made a photo album of all the pictures we made in the last two years together. Under each one, we wrote a funny story about what happened. In the end, we added some drawings Lara made for Brian about our little family and mostly about him and her. She was happy for him, but she cried a lot when it was time for him to leave. They grew on each other, and I was afraid this might happen. The guest room was back to its original look. Empty cupboards, tidy bed, only decorative picture, no clothes all over the place. It still smelled like somebody just left the room, but he was gone. I cleaned the room as Brian took his last boxes away. When he got back, we already prepared everything for our last evening. He opened the door and just froze, seeing us all there with decoration and Lara looking at him so excited with her present in her hands.

"Aww. Thanks, guys." – he walked over and hugged Lara and kneeled down to be on the same level with her. She hugged him and handed over his present.

"Mommy and I made you something to remember us." – she then stepped back and hugged me by the hip. I placed my hand on her face and felt her tears running down her cheeks. I bent down and kissed her on the top of her head.

"He will not forget us, sweety. Brian will still come and watch movies. Right?" – I looked at Brian with a sign it was time for him to explain.

"Of course. We still have so many movies to watch. Your mommy also needs free nights." – he looked up at me, looking for approval.

"Come on, let's have some food, and you can show us what you got." – said Ramos and we went out to the terrace for the food.

Brian sat on the head of the table and opened his present. He looked so touched like I had never seen him before. He had a smile on his face the whole time as he went from one page to another. When he got to the funny parts, he laughed out loud. Even though all of us were talking, he seemed to be in another World. The cheeky, womanizer boy who I knew was gone. He finally grew up and realized he had another type of family. A child, he cared for more than himself and loved like his own. A person who changed his life 180 degrees. He looked at me and said thank you without a single tone only with his lips when he finished. Then he stood up, gave Lara a kiss, whispered something in her ear and left the terrace. I followed him with my eyes only but didn't move. The rest of the evening was full of laughter, stories, and of course, we also watched a movie, where Ramos, Brian and I continued drinking wine. When Jake and Lara went to sleep, Brian left. It was only Lara and me again.

Soon after Brian left, Ramos and I decided to move in together. It was the right time, and also the kids were ready for it. We changed the guest room to Jake's room. He didn't want any new color, just some pictures, and many toys. Ramos and I decided to rent his flat out on Airbnb. He was dealing with cleaning and welcoming guests. Even though his business occupied him a lot, he had some spare time dealing with hospitality. Nate and Ramos got along very well. Christmas and the other holidays were a bit weird, as we had Nate over as well as Brian in the evening. Both of them were known for bringing a plus one. The first one we still remembered, but soon we realized it was always another one, and we didn't bother anymore with names. For me, it seemed like the two of them had a competition over who would bring the better girl. They were mostly models, or some skinny waitress, who didn't have a lot of qualities besides being pretty. I was very glad to have all of them in one place, laugh and have fun together. We were a weird family, but it was us.

Lara and Jake were already eleven years old and started to be real teenagers. Jake and Ramos already had "the talk" about sex and boy stuff, as well as Lara and I. We both wanted it to do it separately, and apparently, we told completely opposite things. Jake and Lara discussed it and told us we don't have a lot of common in our stories. I wondered if it was the topic we told differently or what it means in general. It didn't bother me until I overheard Jake talking to Ramos about a girl he seems to like, and he told him to go for it, and he can always pass on her if she is not good. I was making the bed while Ramos had a shower, and I thought it was the perfect time to ask what he said to Jake.

"Hey. I was wondering what you told Jake about sex."

"General stuff. Nothing much." – he replied while closing the tap and getting out of the shower.

"Interesting. Lara told me you told him to be a womanizer." – he didn't respond until he got to the bedroom with a towel around his waist.

"Well, that too. I mean he has to experience until he finds the one. Like I did" – he came close to me and gave me a kiss.

"So you told him to sleep around? Are you crazy?" – I put his hands down from my waist and stepped back. – "No wonder they got a different story. I told Lara just the opposite. I don't want my girl to be the one who sleeps around with anyone and thinks that it's alright to be kicked out by a boy who gets bored of her." – I crossed my hands and started to get angrier and angrier.

"Wow, Babe. Calm down. I just want to give him a clear picture that it's not good to have one partner no experience." – he changed to his PJ's in the meantime, while I stood and looked at him furiously.

"You can't forget, Lara is a girl, and they share everything. If he tells her that it's okay, she will double-check with me. What is wrong with maybe finding the one soon and not at

30? Having one happy marriage and kids without divorce and fights? Is that such a dream?"

"Well, you also slept with the first guy who came along." – I slapped him in the face once he said that. My eyes filled with tears.

"This just means you don't know me at all." – I said while going out of the bedroom.

"Tess. I didn't mean it…" – he shouted behind me, but I didn't hear the rest. I went into Lara's room and saw her sitting up on the bed as I entered.

"Are you alright, mom?" – she looked at me with sleepy eyes.

"Sorry to wake you, honey. I just wanted to cuddle." – I sat next to her bed, but she moved and placed her hand on the sheets for me to get in. I laid next to her and touched her face and gave her a big kiss on the hand. I closed my eyes, and tears ran down my face. Lara had her eyes closed and a small smile on her face. I placed my arm around her and fell asleep almost instantly. In the morning, when I opened my eyes, I saw Lara looking at me and exploring my face.

"Morning, honey." – I whispered.

"Mom?"

"Yes?"

"Are you happy?" – Lara asked, and I opened my eyes widely and looked at her.

"I am. Why are you asking?"

"I heard you yesterday. Jake and I have a different thought about it. Don't worry." – I smiled and hugged her close to me.

"You are such a clever girl. I never wanted you to do something out of your comfort zone. One day you will understand." – I didn't let her go until she moved away and looked at me with a smile.

"I love you, mom. I want you to be happy." – she touched my heart so deeply every time she said it.

I never believed my mom when she told me what it feels like to be a mother, the feeling you have in your stomach when you don't hear from your child, or the feeling you have when you worry. The moment they kiss you or tell you 'I love you' is the most touching. My heart drops and beats every time. I am filled with happiness whenever I see her smile, laugh, or tell me these three words. When Lara was born, I was so worried about not being good enough and relied on Nate to help me out and be there, but that also changed. He was indeed a great father, but he was not there for me in the way I had hoped he would. I needed a shoulder to cry on, on my hardest days. Someone to remind me that it is all going to be alright or to support me in fights. I thought Ramos was the right person to be there for me, but somehow recently, I started to doubt that. We had been together over four years, and his comment made me wonder if he actually knew the real me. Maybe, even I didn't know who I was. The Tess I knew changed and grew so much since Lara was part of her life. When I looked in the mirror, I wondered a lot of times if there was actually a real Tess. Is that a girl who looked for real love since she was a teenager, or perhaps a hopeless romantic, or even a person being blinded by her kindness?

By the time I got ready to take Jake and Lara to school, Ramos was already gone. As we parked the car, I saw Joanna had just arrived as well with her children. As soon as I stopped the car, Jake and Lara ran away. I walked over to Joanna, whose children did the same.

"Are you free for a coffee?" – I asked her.

"Always. We can have a walk, what do you say?" - she

locked the car and lead the way to a nice coffee shop around the corner from the school. We took the coffees and started to walk around the area.

"How are things with Ramos? Are you getting along?" – Joanna asked.

"Yeah, sure." – I took a sip of coffee. – "Well… Actually…we had a fight yesterday, and I kind of slapped him." – Joanna looked at me with a huge smile and laughed.

"Sounds interesting. Wanna talk about it?"

"We told the kids about sex a few weeks ago. Then Lara told me that we had a completely different story, and it felt a bit weird. I didn't want to ask anything until I heard Jake and Ramos talking about passing on a girl if you don't like her, which made me wonder what he told him in the first place."

"Why didn't you do it together in the first place?" – Joanna asked curiously.

"Well. We thought it would be easier if it was separated between gender, like me talking about period and Ramos about the penis and stuff." – I blushed and looked down.

"I understand that. We also did it separately, but both of us were there. Anyways. What did he say? Did you ask him?"

"Yes. He basically told him to experience more before settling for one girl. It sounded like sex means nothing. Which is maybe a man thing, but Jake tells everything to Lara. I don't want her to sleep around and be the whore of the class later or to be pushed into something she is not ready for."

"You worry too much, Tess. Lara is a smart girl, and whatever you tell her, she will do what she thinks is the best. She is just like you. I am more worried about you."

"It's the last comment that he said." – I stopped for a big breath. – "He told me I slept with the first guy who came along. It sounded harsh and mean. I told him my past, without names, but he knew." – I felt just sad and hurt as I told Joanna the story.

"Talk to him. Maybe he didn't mean it that way, but he deserved the slap for sure." – she hugged me tight and tapped on my back, showing she completely understood me.

We walked back to the cars while changing the topic to

something happier, like our children. After school, I went to the restaurant, which was packed with people. We added breakfast possibility, which was as busy as dinner. We had mostly egg menus, but there were other options, like waffles or French breakfast. We wanted to please the majority of the visitors by not offering too much, but all the right things, so it is easy to decide. Nate got another sous-chef next to him, who was a young French man. He did most of the breakfast shifts and preparations for dinner, where then Nate took over. His name was Thomas; just with a French pronunciation, it sounded like a different name. After completing university in Paris, he worked in several restaurants where he built up his career. His style was very different to Nates, which might be due to the age difference. He was a few years younger than me, but those years were enough to make him very innovative and have a very hipster style. He liked many colors on the plate and used molecular culinary to create the decoration. The whole team liked working with him. He had the music on in the kitchen and made jokes the whole time. Some thought they cannot take him very seriously, but then when something was wrong, he changed and became this strict angry Frenchman. During his interview, I was blinded by his nice blue eyes. I could barely focus. Nate was kicking me under the table to focus and ask more specific questions. When I walked into the restaurant, Thomas was alone in the office and turned towards the entrance as soon as he heard me walking through the kitchen.

"Morning, everyone." – I said loudly, and everybody said it back to me while I was going through the stations.

"Morning, Tess." – Thomas stood up from the chair and showed me to my seat. He had his usual chef coat and black pants on. His blond hair was always in style, and he never took his eyes off mine while speaking to me. He showed me absolute respect but starring for so long made me often very uncomfortable.

"Thanks, Thomas. How is everything? What are the numbers?" – I put my bag on the table and looked at him with an unemotional face.

"Full house. I think you need a waffle today. I'll be right back." – he crossed his hands and raised his eyebrows.

"What makes you say that?" – I stopped and looked up at him.

"You look like you are about to kill somebody, or you just did."

"It's nothing. Didn't sleep well. Sorry. I accept the waffles." - I smiled, and he turned and went straight off to get me breakfast.

The whole day, there was no message, no call or anything from Ramos. It was the first time we'd had a big fight. His way of handling is giving me space or ignoring the fact that I am pretty hurt. Maybe he would surprise me when I got home with some flowers or something. Thomas prepared the best waffles ever. He made on the top a smile face from whipped cream and as he placed the plate in front of he gave we a warming smile.

I picked up Jake and Tess, who were giggling their way towards the car.

"What's so funny, you two?" – I asked as they opened the door and jumped in the backseats.

"Jake kissed a girl," – Lara said while laughing and placing her hand in front of her mouth to hide her giggle.

"Oh. That's…umm…lovely. Who is the girl?" – I asked while starting the engine and getting out of the parking lot.

"Umm… I wanted to kiss Julie, but she pushed me, so I kissed…Ummm… Lara." – they giggled, and it took me by surprise.

"What did you say?"

"It's nothing, mom. It was funny."

I turned back towards the road and thought I will kill Ramos, for telling Jake to be a womanizer and starting with my daughter. I knew that they were teenagers and only fooling around, but I didn't think it was a good idea if Lara and Jake would one day be a thing. It was something I could not control.

When we got home, Ramos was sitting at the kitchen table with a bottle of wine and dinner on the table. He stood up as we entered and greeted me with a smile.

"Are we celebrating?" – Jake asked when he glanced at the table.

"Just being a family," – Ramos replied. – "How was school?" – he looked at Jake, but before he could respond, Lara jumped in.

"We kissed, and mom is angry about it, but it was just funny. What's for dinner?" – Ramos looked at me, but I couldn't look into his eyes. Instead, I walked away to pack away the bags from school.

"I made pasta with some fresh salad. Your mom's

favorite." – Ramos said and followed me into the bedroom.

The kids went to wash their hands and to their rooms before dinner, while Ramos came after me and closed the door of the bedroom behind him.

"Tess... I am sorry... I..." – he started while placing his hand on my shoulder

"I know... Let's just see how it goes..." – I looked at him and left the room to go for dinner.

Ramos knew why I was upset. He knew that we couldn't let a romance between the kids happen; it would destroy the whole concept of our family. It was not only his fault but also mine. We should know better how and what to say to our children. During dinner, Jake and Lara were doing most of the talking, while Ramos and I only laughed and nodded. I never wanted to bring the topic up again. When dinner finished, Ramos got a few calls he didn't pick up. I thought it was very odd and questioned who might call him so late. When the kids went to sleep and I was doing the dishes, I had to ask.

"Why are you not picking up your phone?"

"It's work. I am not sure I want to know what they have to

say." – he continued cleaning up and didn't look up.

"It might be something urgent if they keep calling."

"Let's just leave it. I will talk to them tomorrow."

"What's wrong? Why are you behaving so weird?" – I went over to him and turned him towards me. He just looked down sadly, but before he said something, he looked up and kissed me.

"I got a great offer."

"What kind of an offer?" – I looked surprised.

"A big company offered to buy and expand our product to other countries."

"Wow! That's really great! Why do you make it sound so bad?"

"Because of the other countries part." – He paused and started to walk away to avoid we continue. – "I would have to move away."

Once he said it, I couldn't believe my ears. It was just the absolute opposite of what I expected. He couldn't leave. We couldn't leave. What was going to happen to us? What about the kids? I suddenly had so many unanswered questions going through my mind.

"Where? Why? When?" – I felt tears in my eyes that were ready to slide down my face any second. Ramos heard in my voice that I was getting upset, and he turned back to hug me. He held me tightly and didn't want to let me go.

"If I take it, Jake and even his children will never have to think about money again. The transaction and the preparation will take time... At least one to two years, but then it would mean going to another country thousands of miles away. I can't..."

"Stop." - I hugged him strongly and took a deep breath.

"Tess. I..." – he wanted to interrupt, but I stopped him again.

"You have to do it. I don't know if it will work between us after, but I know you have to do it for Jake. You have to think about his future. He can go to the best university and also do whatever he wants after. Make his own empire and create something great like you did." – I paused and looked down. – "I will wait for you, and we can maybe even figure it out somehow."

"Tess. Since when do long-distance relationships work?"

"I don't know, but I love you, and one or two years extra with you will mean the world to me. I would rather enjoy what's left than think about what's going to happen after." – I placed my head on his shoulder and closed my eyes. That second, all the tears I had been trying to hold back ran down my cheeks.

It was not only about me, but I thought about Lara and Jake. Their friendship and the family we had built. Ramos and I decided not to mention anything to the kids until we knew exactly when they would move away. It might be in a year, but we hoped that it would be two years.

The next day, Ramos called them back from the Restaurant office so I could hear the full deal and accepted the offer. They said that it would be two years until the whole process went through. After Ramos left the office, I asked Brian to take care of the kids in the evening so the two of us could have a romantic dinner and celebrate. Brian never questioned me; he just accepted and was always happy to be with Lara and Jake. During dinner, we discussed a timeline. It was realistic to involve the kids, but it was still far away, so we agreed to enjoy the time and not talk about it until a month before.

Our little family spent every weekend doing something

fun; we travelled the whole summer and spent as much time together as possible. Ramos and I grew together as time passed. We learned a lot about each other and also realized how hard it was going to be to say goodbye or see you later. We avoided the topic, but after two years, Ramos got a call that they had to move in three months, and it was the beginning of their new chapter. Lara and Jake were almost 13 years old. They were difficult teenagers, who were sometimes super moody and hard to talk to. We spent days looking for the best time to talk to them, but one of them always had a problem or was busy with friends. Actually, there was never a good time to tell bad news. Maybe, it gave us a reason to postpone and avoid facing the truth. One night, I got fed up with them being busy and told them they are not allowed to go out; we have to talk.

"Come on, Mom. It's a movie, and I promised…" – Lara started.

"Lara. No." – I snapped.

"But you said promise is…" – Lara continued, but I didn't let her use 'The Promise" against me.

"Lara. I said no. Ramos and I have something to tell you, and we need you both here. We can't postpone it anymore."

We all sat in the living room. On one side of the couch, Ramos and I sat, with the kids just opposite of us.

"Alright, tell us. Maybe I can catch the movie a bit late." – Lara sat down, rolled her eyes and crossed her arms.

"I don't think so." – Ramos started, but then he paused. – "I got a great opportunity in work. A company decided to buy and also expand our product to other regions as well. It all started over two years ago, and we finally finished the paperwork."

"Great, Dad! Are you like a millionaire now?" – Jake smiled and looked excited.

"Something like that, but that's not all."

"As Ramos said, it's also expanding, where they need your Dad to travel there as well." – I continued.

"That's cool. So, he will travel more." - Jake said, but then Lara looked at me and understood there was something more to it. She sat up straight and said.

"You are not telling us something, mom? What's wrong?"

I opened my mouth, but nothing came out. I had no

words to share. I was hurting more than I was showing. I didn't want to let them go.

"I am sorry, kids, but Jake and I will be moving." – said Ramos and placed his arm around me. Once he said it, I swallowed hard and stood up to sit and hug Lara before she got too upset.

"What?" – Lara and Jake shouted out loud, and both started to cry at the same time. I hugged them both.

"We are terribly sorry, but it's all for you." - I said

"How is that good for us? Are you crazy?" – Jake pushed me away and stood up. – "I don't want to leave. Why do you have to destroy everything?" – he looked at Ramos and ran to his room. Ramos wanted to go after him, but Jake locked the door.

"Why, mom? Why?" – Lara sobbed.

"I know you don't understand now, but one day you will. It is the best decision for Jake and also for you. I am terribly sorry, honey. I know you must hate me." – Lara jumped in my lap and hugged me tightly.

"I can never hate you, mom."

Jake didn't talk to us for several days. Lara and Jake spent several nights together on the sofa watching movies and only talking to each other. Lara was also ignoring Ramos and rarely spoke a few words to me. It was going to take them a little time to understand, but we knew they would eventually see why we did it. The flat was packed. The last evening we went all out for a family dinner, where we promised the kids to stay in touch and also that if their friendship is true, it will last no matter what.

Brian came over to drop some papers and saw the house packed. We hadn't told him yet, and he was surprised to see the mess.

"Where are you moving? What did I miss?" - he looked at me, and I just walked over and started crying when I hugged him. – "Tess? What's happening?"

It took me a few seconds to start speaking clearly, but when I did, Brian was even more shocked than the kids.

"Why would you do that? Let him go just like that?" – he asked.

"It's for the kids. I can't let my happiness get in the way of the future Jake could have. It will guarantee him a good life, and that's all I can wish for."

Brian waited for Ramos to come home and speak to him

as well. The two of them talked on the terrace, where both of them looked at me several times.

On the day of the move, Jake and Lara were crying their souls out. Brian came over as well for a farewell and also to pick up the pieces that were left. Ramos and I had our longest kiss ever. I didn't want it to stop. I was holding his shirt tight and holding him close. Lara and Ramos shared a big hug, and he gave her an envelope to open when they leave. We took our last glance at each other, and the door closed. They were gone.

Lara sat on the floor and cried until Brian sat next to her and hugged her. I went to the terrace to take a deep breath. My child needed me. I had to get my shit together and be there for her.

When I walked in, the two of them were still on the floor, and the envelope Ramos gave Lara was on the floor. I picked it up and handed it over to her to open it.

"Would you like to see what's in it?" – even I didn't know what's in it, but maybe it would cheer her up. Lara opened it, and it was a letter from Ramos.

Dearest Lara,

You are all grown up now. When I first met you, you were just a small little girl running towards her mom at school. You showed me love, passion and how a real family should be. I will be grateful for that forever.

I know you don't understand why your mother and I decided this, but one day you will. Your friendship with Jake is special. Cherish it and never let each other go.

Your mother thought this is the best decision for Jake to guarantee him a good future, but you are also mine. I created a bank account for you, which you can use when you are 18 years old. It will be enough for you to pay for the best university, get your first flat and start your life.

You are one of the brightest kids I have met. Use that little brain of yours and you will create big things in World.

We will always love you,

Jake and Ramos

I looked at Brian with an open mouth. I knew Ramos loved both of us, but I never thought I would meet a man who would have such a huge heart to love somebody so much. He believed in her, and it meant the world to me. It was better than any money he left.

CHAPTER 5

The first few days after Ramos and Jake left, the apartment felt empty. Ramos's kind touch, gentle kisses, his accent, which always made me giggle and, of course, the romantic evenings we had together were irreplaceable. I tried my best not to show my sadness in front of Lara, but in some lonely moments, I pushed my head in the pillow and sobbed. There was a night, where I thought Lara was sleeping, but she passed the master bedroom and heard me. The next moment she was all cuddled behind me and holding me close to her.

"I am here, mom. I will never leave you." – she whispered in my ears and made me smile. I held her hand close to me, and we fell asleep.

These moments always brought me back to when I was a teenager and complained about boys or totally unimportant things that made me upset, and my mom would cuddle behind me. When my parents divorced, I had a tough time going through it. Even though I never showed it, I hated my dad for leaving us. He broke us and left the best thing in life – family. There were nights I felt comfortable with my mom in the bed holding me. It gave me so much energy and love that all the hatred I gathered towards my father turned into pity. He lost the most beautiful thing in life, to be loved by someone endlessly. I promised myself, one day, when I have a family, I will do everything in my power to keep it together and give the most I can to my child. Even though my marriage died before Lara could walk, Nate and I had a great relationship. We were like two best friends, and Lara loved that. We mostly argued about the restaurant and cost-saving, but whenever it was about family or how to raise Lara, we were on the same page.

Days slowly turned to months since Jake and Ramos left. As in every long-distance relationship, at the beginning, you call each other as much as possible, but soon it will change to daily, weekly and even fewer calls. One of us was always busy, and we just could not keep it up. The time zone difference was not the only thing that made it difficult, but I realized and Ramos that we had to let go slowly. If we really thought we would make it together, we would find our way back.

Lara and Jake were still texting all the time, and even after three years, nothing changed. Their teenage years were at their peak, and it was time to figure out where to apply for university. For me, it was also a mental preparation that she might want to move away. For her 16th birthday, I got her a new laptop, and it was the perfect way to start a topic that she should maybe start looking around schools. We kept the birthday low key by only inviting family, and of course, Brian. I organized a separated area for us in the restaurant and made the Lara special menu, which was also known as the children menu we offered. Nate wanted to change it all the time, but Lara didn't let him because it was her ultimate favorite. Starting with a tomato soup, main course fusilli with cream and ham, and the dessert was a tiramisu glass. We made this menu when Lara was 8. Every child loves it, and the kitchen is also fond of it.

We left home and picked Nate and Brian on the way there to go in one car. Steve was coming with his family and picked mom up on the ride over. When we arrived, the whole staff was there and all of them were holding a pink balloon. Lara's smile was until her ears; she was so happy and surprised to see them all.

"Wow. This looks so awesome! Thank you, guys! I love it!" – Lara said and started to hug every employee one by one.

We arrived at the same time with the other car, and of course, Jessie and Vincent ran out of Steve's car to greet

Lara first. The real adults went more for the drinks.

"Would you like to drink or drive?" – I bent over to Brian, but Nate interrupted us.

"I'll drive; I have a date in the evening and have to make myself presentable." – he added

Brian and I just exchanged a look and started the interrogation.

"Who is she?" – I asked

"Maybe it's a he.." – Brian added, but I slapped his lap.

"I don't kiss and tell." – Nate responded and took a sip from his water.

"That we know…" – I rolled my eyes. – "Tinder date or somebody requested the chef, and it was love at first sight?" – I put my elbows on the table and held my chin with my hand to look excited to hear the story.

"Leave the man alone, sis. He should have fun. Go for it. Maybe he can teach you how to go out again." - Steve added as Nicole and he joined us at the table.

"Thanks, mate." – Nate raised the glass at Steve, and he nodded.

"You are all still like teenagers. I just heard the kids talking about dates, and here I am at the adult table and the same topic. Don't you have anything else to talk about?" – Mom came over and sat next to me. I smiled at her and bent my head, showing understanding. She was absolutely right, but except Steve and Nicole, all of us were single; we actually didn't have anything else to talk about.

"So, did you have the talk about university and where Vincent would like to go?" – I asked Steve

"We didn't need to, he came to us and told us he would like to go to the London Business School. Which was actually great, as it was also the school I really wanted to attend, so at least he can enjoy it instead of me." – Steve responded while looking over toward Vincent with proudness in his eyes.

"That's so great, my dear. Which course will he take?" – Mom asked

"International Business. He is already putting his head together with a few of his mates to do an app, which will change the online payment world. Don't ask us more, because he is all about programming and how much money he will make."

"Jessie is thinking about hospitality and going towards Hotel Management, but she still has time to change her mind. She might do a summer internship first to see if she likes it or not." – added Nicole.

"You guys have it all planned out. It's really amazing." – I paused and took a deep breath. – "I still haven't talked about it with Lara, but hopefully soon, so I can prepare myself.". Everybody laughed and knew that I deeply just wanted to keep her as close as possible and never let her go.

The children joined us, and the food came one after the other. We barely had time to breathe or talk. When we finished, it was time for the presents. Steve and Nicole got Lara a great weekend trip with Jessie and Vincent during the summer for a long weekend. Brian was not creative, so he gave her a two-year Netflix membership. Nate and I gave her a new Apple Macbook, and we used the time to also start the university topic.

"Happy Birthday, my love. I hope you will use it for good and also maybe even for your university applications." – Nate said. He handled it quite direct, and we were all surprised to hear that.

"Thank you both. It's great. I love it. Yes… university and

stuff." – Lara said, lowering her voice when it came to school. I just exchanged a worrying look with Nate.

After the presents, we packed all the presents into the car. When I hugged Steve, he whispered in my ear.

"Don't push her. She knows what she wants. She will come to you; just be patient and relax. She will for sure go to university, but she has plenty of time." – we smiled, and I nodded at him. – "Love you, sis. Keep me posted."

Nate drove Brian home first, then us. He changed to his car, and off he was to his date.

"What would you like to do, birthday girl? Movie night, or should we do something more fun?" – I put our stuff down on the kitchen counter and looked excited at Lara, who was standing shyly at her room entrance.

"Movie sounds fun, but can I ask you something?" – she kept her hands behind her back and looked uncomfortable talking.

"What's wrong, honey? Tell me anything. Is this about Dad's comment about university? There is no pressure. You can choose whatever you want to do. We have time."

"No. It's alright. It's actually about that. I have an idea, but

I don't know if you would like it." - she started to walk towards me and placed several brochures on the table, which she hid behind her.

"Let's hear it. I am sure we can figure it out." – I smiled and turned the brochures towards me. It was all hospitality, cooking, baking, hotel and restaurant management. What's there to worry about? I would love her to do the same thing I did and to take over the restaurant one day. It would be a dream come true to me.

"I would like to go with Jake to the Cornell University in New York," – she said it so fast that I barely understood it.

"That's one of the best universities in the world. I finished my master's there. That's so great. I am totally happy for you, darling. I only hope you are not doing this for Jake." – I smiled at her.

"It was our plan all along. The time to be together and enjoy the missed years. We wanted it like that." – her voice was full of excitement

"If you have a real friendship, then no distance can change that. You don't have to go to the same university for that. Please do what you want and where you want it. Love is important, honey, but don't give up your dreams for it." –

I tried to be understanding, but it wasn't what she wanted to hear. Her face changed to an unreadable one, and she looked down.

"Brian told me you would say something like this." – she said and stood up. Wait. Brian knew? He played a fool today, he never said anything. I could kill him now.

"Brian? What do you mean?" – I crossed my arms and stood up to level her.

"I told him cause I was worried about your reaction. I knew he would know how and when to talk to you. He said, you will be upset about the Jake part, and you will give me this life lecture about friendship and love. He was right, but you are not." – she took all the brochures and stormed off to her room.

"Lara, come back to talk. I just don't want you to…."

"Make the same mistake you did?" – she interrupted and left me speechless. The next thing I heard was her slamming the door, and I was left in the kitchen like a fool. I took my phone out and texted Brian.

I hate you. You kept me in the dark? I was telling you everything, and you listened and didn't say anything. Why? Why? You knew I was stressed out about this university thing…. I hate you.

I placed my phone on the counter and went to Laras' room and knocked. I didn't want to destroy her birthday with an argument. I wanted to let her know I was completely on her side.

"Lara? Can I come it?" – I asked while opening the door. To my surprise, she was lying on the bed, hugging her favorite fluffy Obelix she got from Nate from Disneyland and crying in the dark. I walked over to her and sat on the floor to face her.

"I am sorry, sweetheart. I never wanted to upset you. I am supporting you in every decision and will be by your side whatever you choose. I know you think I missed something in my life, and I regret it, but I don't. I have you, and you are the most wonderful gift one could ever wish for. Your grandma gave up her university for love and followed her love, your grandfather. That's how Steve and I were born. I asked her many times if she would change anything or regrets her decision. Her answer was clear as ice. Never. I would never stop you from following your dreams or your love. I want what is best for you. Brian might be right in many things, but in one thing, he isn't. I never lost my love; I found it when I held you in my arms." – tears ran down my cheeks and I swallowed hard to keep myself together.

"I love you, mom. I will never do something crazy like that. I want to have my own place and build my career like you did. I loved all your hotel stories which you told me before sleeping. Thank you for having my back." - she hugged me, and I closed my eyes. At that moment, all the tears I held back came out. When we let go, I cleaned her and my face and smiled at her while cupping her face.

"We have had enough of crying for tonight. What do you say, you go out with friends to celebrate, and we can do a movie and crying another time?" - I told her to cheer her up.

"With hot cocoa?" – Tess added.

"What else." – I winked at her and helped her get out of bed. She texted all her friends, and in a few minutes, the party was on. As I went to leave to let her get ready, she took me by the hand.

"Stay. Help me get ready." – There was no response needed. I turned back and sat on her bed.

We spent at least an hour changing into several dresses, laughing about the stuff she wanted to put on. I did her hair while she was doing her make-up. We chose a short black dress with a spaghetti strap on one side, and the back was looser, so you could see a bit of meat but not too much. I curled her hair, and she put on nice light makeup with a pink lipstick. When she was done, she walked around the room like she was in a fashion show.

"I think you missed one thing. Wait here." – I went to my garderobe and took out one of my oldest pair of high heels. It was the shoes I had at my graduation. They were still comfortable, and the heel was not that high; I thought it is the perfect shoe for a beginner. – "Try them on." – I placed the shoes in front of her, and she slipped her feet into them. They were a perfect fit, just like Cinderella.

"They are really pretty, mom." – she turned towards the mirror.

"My graduation shoes. It was time to pass them to you."

"The one you barely wore, when Brian was carrying you?" – we laughed.

"Well, maybe you will be lucky, and somebody will carry you one day. Have fun, honey. I will drive you, alright?" – we stood for a second and looked at the mirror. She would always be my baby, but she was more of a woman now.

I took my phone and bag, and we were already in the car. Again. I drove her to a friend's place. Lara got out of the car, but before she closed the door, she turned and said.

"Thank you, mom, for everything. I love you."

"Take care and call me if you need me to pick you up. Otherwise, please call a cab. Have fun!" – I shouted after her.

I sat in the car and checked my phone. I got a message from Brian, but before I get annoyed, I texted Steve.

You were right. She came to me right after the party. NY it is! Cornell University. Seems we did a good job bro. Thanks for stopping me from annoying her. Love you!

Let's see what stupid thing Brian has to say. Another excuse probably that he wanted to protect me, and it was not his place to tell.

I am sorry. I promised her not to tell you. How are you?

That's it? Alright, I was just going to ignore it. I drove home and opened a bottle of wine, and started my research. How far is New York? Best places to live? Most dangerous places to live? Tuition fees and other fees. I was actually happy that Jake would be there for her. I took my phone to write to Ramos, but then I changed my mind. Maybe he doesn't know it yet. Then I saw an Instagram post from Jake in front of Cornell with the comment – 'Can't wait to start here. Thank you, dad!'. I took my phone to write to Ramos; maybe he already knew the answers to my questions.

Congratulations on Cornell! I am happy the kids decided to stay together and continue their dream TOGETHER. I am doing my research now about it. I saw you went to New York with Jake? How did you like it?

As I sent the message, somebody rang on the door. I

wasn't expecting any guests, and I already had my bottle of wine, which made me a bit tipsy and not in the mood for chatting. I checked the door, and it was Brian.

"What are you doing here?" – I asked through the closed door.

"Let me in. I want to talk." – he shouted

I closed my eyes and paused, then opened the door for him and went back to the kitchen to check my phone. Brian closed the door behind him and came after me to sit on the bar next to the kitchen counter. As I took the phone in my hand, I saw Ramos' response, but decided to face Brian first and then check it out. I looked up at Brian with my eyebrows up and hands crossed.

"So what do you want to say?" - I demanded.

"She came to me for help, and I couldn't say no. I didn't know you didn't know about it until the end, she asked me to keep it a secret. It was not my place to get between you nor be the one to tell you that you have a clever daughter who made a great choice. I thought you knew that by yourself."

"So… I should thank you for saying I am against it cause I had some crush and missed out on something." – I attacked back

"No. I know you made the right choices, but as smart as you are, you are not giving the right judgement now. I tried to help, and you shouldn't be mad at me. I think you should be happy and supportive. That's all. I know it will be hard for you when she leaves, but... hey... Nate, Steve, Nicole, your mom are all here for you.... As am I." – Brian took my hand and poured me some more of the wine.

"I know. I am sorry. I just thought she would come to me instead of you. Not even Nate... " – I took a sip from the wine and looked over my phone, which got another message. – "Let me check my phone. Lara is out; maybe she needs something. Would you like to watch a movie?" – I asked while taking the phone and looking down. I isolated myself into a bubble and couldn't hear the response. The message was from Ramos.

Hey Tess! Good to hear from you. I am super proud, as I assume you too. They deserve the best.

A few minutes later, another message.

I am sorry about the picture… I wanted to tell you, but it was never the right time.

Another message right after that.

Let's talk about it. She is just a friend, nothing serious…

My jaw dropped. What picture? What girlfriend? I opened Jake's Instagram, and only then I saw there were more pictures. The last one was the three of them. Three… Who is she? Why is she with them? How is this possible? Why am I the last one to know about anything? I clicked on her profile and checked her out. She had several pictures, all were of her kissing Ramos on some beach and fancy restaurants. The oldest was from two months ago. How could he keep me in the dark for so long? I assumed Lara knew; she probably didn't want to upset me. Everybody tries to protect me by not telling, but it hurts even more when I find out they are lying. I hope one day they will understand this.

"Tess? .. Hey.. do you hear me?" – Brian's face popped in front of mine. I looked up, and my eyes were just filled with tears. The pain of being heartbroken just hit me. I couldn't feel my legs anymore. My legs were shaking, my chest was tight, and all I wanted to do was burst into tears. - "What's wrong?" – I just gave the phone to Brian without saying anything and took the whole bottle of wine and started to drink. Brian started to read the message and to check her profile, then saw me drink up the whole bottle.

"Hey, who cares about this guy? He left you three years ago… he doesn't deserve a tear from you." - he threw my phone on the kitchen counter and deleted all the messages from Ramos, so I never had to look at them again. He was right; we separated a long time ago. He didn't owe me any explanation of who is he dating or sleeping with. It still hurt and annoyed me.

"She is so beautiful…. I could never be like that… her legs… did you see that body?" – my head started to spin, and I could barely talk.

"Look at me, you idiot. You are the most amazing person I know. Who cares about that supermodel? She is a girl you take home for a spin; you are the type you introduce to your parents." – he kissed my forehead, and I smiled. – "Come. Let's make you a nice cold bath to freshen up."

"I don't want to go anywhere with you." – I jumped up from the stool and started to run away, but I didn't get far. I felt like a little child playing around. It was probably a worse sight than a small child, more like an alcoholic running away from the police after she stole liquor from the store. Brian caught me and picked me up and placed me on his shoulder. Once I turned upside down, the world started spinning even more. I closed my eyes and passed out. The next minute I woke up, I was sitting in a cold bath, and my head was wet. I must have woken up to the cold water, which was splashed on my face. There were bubbles everywhere, and Brian was sitting on a chair opposite of me.

"Jesus. I am naked. What are you doing here?" – I shouted and try to hide my body from him.

"How do you think you got here?" – he smiled and started laughing at me. He gave me a small mirror to show my face. I looked like a panda. My makeup was all everywhere. First, I got angry, but then I just started laughing at myself.

"I am sorry. I am pretty much a mess. Sorry for this and for being mad at you. The wine I had was too much." - I apologized and looked down at the bubbles.

"You just had two bottles. No wonder. I'll bring you an aspirin, so you don't have a headache tomorrow. If you are still in the mood, we can turn on a movie in your bedroom, and you can fall asleep, and then I will leave and lock up." – he stood up and opened the medicine drawer to look for some aspirin.

"You can sleep here. No need to run away. We can have breakfast tomorrow with Lara if you want." – I added and took the towel to dry myself. Brian was still and turned away from me to give me privacy. It felt a bit weird, but somehow it was also alright. It was like a cousin looking over me. Nothing weird about that.

We went to the master bedroom and turned on the first Netflix rom-com we saw. It was something we didn't really have to pay attention, and I could easily fall asleep, but I didn't. I was thinking about Ramos and the woman. I felt heartbroken and wanted to feel needed and loved again.

Brian was sitting on the bed, and I was lying on his side under his arm. We didn't move through the whole movie. He sometimes looked down to see if my eyes were closed, but I just looked up and smiled at him. I don't remember what went through my head, but I knew I needed a distraction. I slowly got up from his side and looked at him.

"Are you alright?" – he asked. I moved towards him and sat in his lap.

"Just keep quiet." – I placed a finger on his mouth and kissed him. Without any hesitation, he kissed me back, and our tongues touched. His hands were all over my waist, and he moved me slowly on him. We stopped for a breath, and he asked.

"Tess... Are you..." – I didn't want to talk. I wanted a distraction and the feeling to be touched. He turned me over to my back and came on top of me, never letting go of my mouth. My heart was beating faster and faster. I could feel the goosebumps, the inner feeling of excitement and the feeling I missed so much. A warm kiss, a sensitive touch, a passionate romance and my brain turned off.

We laid next to each other naked, pillows on the floor around us, both of our chests moving up and down, the film almost ending in the background, there was no movement, no word, but then a door opening broke the moment. Lara was home. She couldn't see this, it would confuse her.

"Get dressed fast." – I ordered and jumped up to pick up the pillows and dress up. – "Where is my nightgown?" – I asked, and Brian handed it to me while standing naked and moving slowly to the bathroom. I took a late glance at his back, which made me smile for a second.

"I'll take a shower." – he added through the closed door.

I just sat back in the bed and tied my hair up when Lara entered the room.

"I saw the light and knew you are up. It was such an awesome night." – she said loudly, with a huge grin on her face. She placed her bag by the door and jumped into the bed. – "I met this boy and…." – she stopped and turned toward the bathroom. "Who is that?"

"It's just Brian. We were watching a movie, he came over. So, who is the boy?" – I looked excitedly.

"Hey Brian." – Lara shouted and then turned back to me. – "So, we went out and danced, and there was this boy. Tall, blond and gorgeous blue eyes. We danced together and then he was gone for a few minutes. He came back out of the blue and kissed me. It was so good. I saw stars. Everybody was screaming, but I couldn't hear anything. It was like in a fairytale. We then decided to go home, and even though he lives in the other part of the city, he walked me home and asked me out tomorrow." – she blushed, and happiness was written all over her face.

"That's so nice, sweety. Your first boyfriend. That's so exciting. When is the date?"

"He said he will text me tomorrow. I hope you don't mind." – she looked down with her puppy eyes.

"It's your day with your dad, so you have to tell him." – I smiled. That was going to be interesting. Nate would probably freak out. First the university and then a boyfriend. Poor fella. I think he will not expect that kind of a day tomorrow.

"Well…What if you tell him?" – I turned my head to the side and raised my eyebrows. She knew that's a big no from my side. – "Alright. I'm going to sleep. See you tomorrow." – she kissed me and jumped up from the bed, and left the room.

I was still unable to move. This day was packed with too many happenings, and I still felt dizzy from the wine. Brian got out of the shower with a towel around his waist, and just as he was about to come back to the bed, Lara opened the door and came in.

"Wow. That's so much skin there." – she covered her face, and Brian grabbed my bathrobe to cover up. – "I was just wondering if you are sleeping together or how come you used this bathroom. It's a bit odd…" – She put down her hands and waited for an explanation. Would this be the first time I lie to her?

"We were…" – Brian started, but I interrupted him and continued.

"We were watching a movie, and I was too lazy to clean the other shower, so I told him to use this one. He will sleep in the guest bedroom. I'll go and make it." – Brian looked at me then down. I jumped from the bed and went over to Lara to take her out of the room.

"I already thought you were a thing… It would be weird, but also pretty awesome. Well, maybe in another lifetime." – she added and turned away to go back

"We? No. That's never going to happen, you know that." – I said and walked her back to her room to make sure she stays there this time. When I turned, Brian was all dressed up and picking up his things to leave.

"Where are you going?" – I asked and walked over to him.

"I am leaving Tess." – he said and just left without letting me say another word.

What just happened? Did I miss something or say something? I actually didn't know. I went back to the bedroom to sleep, but before I did, I wrote Brian.

What just happened?

As I placed the phone on the bedside table, it vibrated. New message.

You honestly said what you think.

CHAPTER 6

I didn't know what to respond to Brian's message and left the conversation with that. I needed a good night's sleep and also a new day with fewer surprises.

Lara left early to go to Nate's and spend the day with him. At least that was the original plan, but she had her first date well. I spent the day drinking three coffees and planning events in the restaurant. I finished a few emails and was ready to leave when Lara and Nate came home.

"I'll be right out. Thanks, dad." – she said and went to her room.

"Hey. What are you doing back? I was just about the leave." – I turned, surprised to see them.

"Well, our daughter just ditched me for her boyfriend, and I told her I will take her wherever she is going." – he said and took a seat next to me.

"Are you stalking the poor boy?" – I smiled, and he looked at me.

"When did she become so big?" – he looked at me terrified.

"Hey. It's all going to be fine. Come to the restaurant after and you can help me. It will get your thoughts away. Plus, we have to talk about the university stuff."

"I forgot how much of a control freak you are. I missed that." - he added, and just as I wanted to reply, Lara got out of the room all dressed up with full make-up on, ready to go.

"You look beautiful!" – Nate and I said it at the same time as we saw our little baby girl all grown up.

Lara was all head over heels about the boy. Nate met him on the first date and said he was a well-raised boy with good manners. Dating and going out became part of every weekend; we barely had time to spend with her, instead, we had Nate and Tess dates in the restaurant. We prepared the budget for the next year, did all the administration, looked for some new hires, tried to catch up with all the marketing campaigns, and invent new meals. Nate shared his date stories, where I just laughed at how many weird people he met. It was like two best friends having fun. Except, the real best friend I had still wasn't talking to me.

"What's up with Brian? You haven't mentioned him for a long time." – Nate asked one day.

"I don't know. We haven't spoken for a month now." – I couldn't look him in the eye and start the whole topic.

"That's a new thing. What did you do?" – He asked with a cheeky smile.

"What makes you think it's my fault?" – I turned to him and crossed my arms.

"I was married to you, and I have a child with you. I kind of know you, Tess. You are kind of a control freak, and sometimes you mess it up, and you need time to bring yourself back to balance. It's like the time you wanted to arrange a garden party for Laras' 5th birthday, and it was raining, and you almost had a mental breakdown, even though we actually had a Plan B." – he continued looking at recipes while telling me it my fault without knowing what really happened.

"I wanted to have a perfect day for my daughter. Is that such a big thing to ask?" – I shocked my head and continued reading the recipe, but Nate closed it in front of me and turned back to face me.

"Tell me what happened." – he sat up on the kitchen table, ready to listen. Maybe he wasn't ready to hear everything, but it might be a good solution to tell him and get a second opinion. I started with the university fight with Lara and all the way until I got my last message from Brian. Nate was smiling most of the time and somehow didn't seem so surprised to hear about it. Which annoyed me in some way.

"I will not tell you what you did wrong, but I know you will understand it one day. I will give you a few more years to think about it. If you don't know it by your 45th birthday, I will tell you." – he jumped off the table and grinned.

"Why? Why don't you seem surprised? I was ready for a speech from you and a big lesson on how many mistakes I made, how stupid I am." – I wanted his help and his anger and telling me I made a mistake. Why didn't he say it?

"You are a big girl, Tess. I know everything happens for a reason. Us meeting, having a great daughter, her leaving for a great university. It will give you big freedom and maybe loosen you up a bit. You are too uptight and only think about her. I think it's time to think what you will do when Lara leaves." – he walked out the door and left me to think. I was frozen. I didn't move for a few minutes and just thought about everything he said. I was still in a stage where I didn't know the answers to what he said. My life was Lara. I woke up to make her day and be there for her. This had been my life for over 16 years. I couldn't just change it. A mother will always be attached to her children, even when they are 30 and might have their own family.

It was already over a month of Lara seeing Daniel and I thought it was time to meet him as well, so I suggested that he came over for dinner. Lara was very happy about the idea. She invited Nate to meet him properly and took over the kitchen to do everything herself. We spent the whole afternoon cooking and baking with her. She wanted to be the one doing everything, so Nate and I were only drinking wine and watching over her. It was adorable to see her move around the kitchen like a good housewife. As she spent most of her childhood in the restaurant and in the kitchen, there was no need to help; she knew her way around spices, serving, when to put something in the oven, how to make the perfect pastry or her favorite Tiramisu. Nate and I were there for some additional help to cut things or to wash up. She was quite strict and didn't let us try anything until it was completely done. Half an hour before Daniel came, Lara went to change, while Nate and I used the time to try everything. As both of us were perfectionists, we wanted to have the best meal. We took two little spoons and went through each meal without saying anything. The way she twisted some spices in the lasagna emphasized the taste of homemade tomato sauce. Instead of instant coffee, she added Columbian quality coffee in the Tiramisu. It was a whole other level. Everything was simply amazing. Even better than either of us could do.

"So, what do you think?" – Lara said from behind us.

"Honey, we are speechless. The flavors are amazing. You did a great job. That New York school of yours will be happy to have you." – Nate said and hugged her. I joined all his thoughts with a nod. All of us took the spoon and started to taste another round. The doorbell was the only reason we stopped. Lara ran over to open the door. It was Daniel. He was a head taller than Lara, had a nicely ironed white shirt with navy green pants and black shoes. His clothing style was good, and his hair was pretty much perfect. He looked like a small version of Nate. Daniel kissed Lara, took his shoes off and took the guest slippers Lara handed him. In one hand, he had a bag and in the other a beautiful bouquet of flowers. What a nice boy to bring flowers to my daughter. I already liked him. Daniel and Lara walked over to the kitchen where Nate and I were standing and watching them.

"Dad, you already met, but Daniel, this is my mom, Tess."
– Lara introduced us, and I put my hand out to shake and
smiled at him.

"It is nice to meet you. I heard a lot about you. Lara told
me you are a fan of wine, so I brought you something for
the dinner, but as I thought it might be a
misunderstanding, I brought you flowers as well." – he
handed both to me, and he took me by surprise. What a
wonderful boy.

"You are already her favorite." – whispered Lara to Daniel,
who laughed back.

"Lara made all the meal, so if you want, we can start." – I
pointed in the direction of the table.

"Let's wait a few more minutes." – Lara interrupted.

"Alright. Won't the meal get cold?" – Nate said and looked
at me for answers, which I didn't have. As a chef, Nate
would never let a meal get cold, but this time it was not
just the meal we had to wait for. It was something else.

"We are still waiting for…." – Lara started, but then the
doorbell rang again. She ran over to open it and to my
utmost surprise, it was Brian. She hugged him, and he gave
her a kiss on the cheek.

"So where is that boy of yours?" – he asked and handed her a nice flower. Daniel walked over to introduce himself. Without any handshake, he hugged the boy like they were old friends. – "Hey guys." – he added, looking over Nate and me.

Nate walked over to me and whispered to me.

"I assume you didn't know he was coming."

"No, but let's open that wine." – I went to the kitchen and took out the cutlery and plates for Brian to place on the table, as well as an additional wine glass.

"Now we can eat." – Lara said, and they all went to the dining table, except Brian, who came to me.

"Let me help you." – he said.

"What are you doing here? You ignore me for weeks, and you come just like this and pretend everything is ok. Why are you not talking to me?" – I attacked him but kept my voice down.

"Lara invited me. I would never say no to her. Let's eat." – he took the plates from my hands and took them to the table.

I drank the remaining wine in my glass and walked over

with a fake smile on my face, which Nate saw with concerned eyes.

"So, I wanted you all to be here and try the full meal I made, which is even better than what we serve in the restaurant and also meet Daniel." - Lara took her glass for a toast, and we followed her.

"I am proud of you, baby." – Daniel said and dug into the food.

The dinner was full of awkward moments when Lara asked something from Brian and me, and none of us really wanted to speak, so Nate jumped in. I tried to only smile and nod and ask questions from Daniel to get to know him better. Deep within my soul, I was irritated about Brians' presence, and it made me anxious. Daniel was a very nice boy, he showed interest toward all of us, and spoke a lot about his family, plans and also how he likes spending time with Lara. He was also open about going to Dubai to continue his studies at the NYU campus there. Before we would ask what would happen to them, they looked at each other and said openly.

"As we will study on the other side of the planet, we decided to take a break and maybe Daniel can change campus for the second year." - Lara answered and shocked us all at how forward planning they were.

When the dinner ended, Lara and Daniel went for a walk, while Nate, Brian and I stayed to clean up. I got a ping on my phone, and it was an unexpected notification.

Your ovulation day is coming.

An app I used to follow my period. Good to know. I cleared the note, and as I put the phone on the table, it hit me. Wait. When did I have my period? Shit.

"Can you start cleaning up?" – I shouted over and ran to the bathroom. I started to take the whole bathroom apart to find a pregnancy test. I knew I had one somewhere. I heard somebody coming towards the bathroom.

"Are you alright?" – Brian asked through the door.

"Yeah. Go away. I'll be right there." - I replied and finally found the pregnancy test. At the exact moment I held it up, Brian opened the door and ignored my response.

"Tess…" – he stopped and looked at my hand, holding the test. – "Is that a pregnancy test?"

"I missed my period. I just realized it when I got my reminder on the phone." – I said and unpacked the test. – "Can you leave me please to do it?"

"No. If you are pregnant, then it would be mine. I want to be here." – he placed his hand on mine, but I pulled away and went over to the toilet.

Once I was done, I placed the stick next to the sink and sat on the floor, where Brian joined me.

"Where were you the last month?" – I asked him with a disappointed voice.

"I needed time to think." – he paused then took my hand and turned my face towards his – "Do you think it's a boy or a girl?" – he smiled, and I laughed.

"You are crazy. We are both over 40, this is insane." – I reached up to get the stick to see the result, but before I could, Brian added one last comment.

"It would be a love child."

The next few months, I spent organizing the restaurant event, helping Lara with mock exams, listening to her stories about Daniel and their first fight. She spent each night with me when they fought, and we would watch some romantic movie with nice hot cocoa. Besides all the other things, I had to add a few doctor visits to my list. I think any woman could join me and say they hate going to the gynecologist, and I was one of them. When I got pregnant with Lara, I met a great doctor who was very supportive throughout the whole ride. I went to him every year for a checkup. This time I felt like I was doing the walk of shame. When I got into the office, he stood up from his chair and walked over the shake my hand.

"How are you, Tess?" – his kind smile was the reason I came here the first time.

"I... I am...good. Could you have a check to see if everything is alright?" – I asked and placed my belongings on the chair.

"You sound insecure. Please take off your pants, and let's have a look. Tell me. How is your sex life?" – he showed me to the ordination, and I started to take my pants off while staring at the floor. How should I explain this? I shouldn't say anything and just let it be. I sat up on the chair, and he took a sample first, then prepared everything to do an ultrasound.

"So, these are your ovaries. Both sides look alright and working. Let's see what's in the uterus." – he moved around and only made a "hmm" sound. – "So, it's all good. You are fine; you are reaching earlier menopause."

"I actually missed a period and did a test. It was negative. I thought I should worry." – I stood up and went to dress up.

"You are fine, Tess. Maybe you had intercourse after a long break, and your hormones are still wined up. What do you think?" – he looked at me above his glasses with a smile.

"Yeah. My sex life is sad. I had an unplanned night, and who knows what my body thought." – I sat on the chair opposite of the doctor.

"Your body enjoyed it for sure. Every person needs these hormones, Tess. We are made like this. In your case, the question is what your mind and heart enjoy. I will write you up some pills to make it easier through menopause. Just take one each week, and you will find."

"Thank you." - I stood up and shook his hand.

"Give my regards to Lara. She should also come sometimes before she leaves."

So true. She was also coming here, and he probably knew

about her university and boyfriend. I went to the pharmacy to buy the medicine, and on the way home, I thought about the test. What would have happened if it was positive? Start from square one with a baby? I would never have a day in my life where I was not carrying about a diaper. Just as Lara is about to leave for university and I will try to live a life without her, there would be another child. I couldn't imagine that. Would I raise it alone? How would the whole thing work with Brian? Nate was different. We were married, and I knew he would do anything for her. Even though our marriage didn't last long, he was more an adult in his 20's then now. Brian was always the heartbreaking type who enjoyed more one-night stands. I could not have that around a baby. Maybe he would change. Hmm. He was different with Lara and a great godfather who was supporting her in all her crazy ideas. Well, I would never know.

The year passed by with a blink of an eye. It was already the year of Laras' 18th birthday, my 45th birthday, graduation and Lara moving away from home. We had several events in the restaurant and a potential big business with a startup company to organize their team buildings in the restaurant and summer and Christmas party. The man in charge was very kind through the emails, and I wanted to pass him over to Nate to do the tour and pitch, but he insisted on me, so I let it be. We arranged a tour of the restaurant and a tasting one afternoon. I went there earlier to get everything ready and check with the kitchen if all the meals were ready.

"Hello? Is anybody here?" – said a voice in the restaurant. I took one last glance at the kitchen, and everything was perfect and went out to meet the man. He had a grey suit, dark black hair and brown eyes, which were almost black. He was freshly shaved with a small cut next to the collar. His teeth were white and shining like the black shoes he wore. He had a black folder with him with his laptop inside.

"Hello. You must be Zayn. I am Tess. Nice to meet you." – I reached out for his hand.

"Nice to finally meet you. I was looking forward to our meeting. You have a lovely restaurant here." – he said and looked around.

"Thank you. Actually, my ex-husband Nate did most of the work. That's why I suggested you meet with him. Anyways… let me show you around." – I turned and showed him the way to the terrace first. It was the main reason most people booked us for events, then we went over the glass terrace, which was our second unique selling point. He looked around and stared at me more than anything, which made me uncomfortable. When we went back to the restaurant, the meal was already prepared on one of the tables.

"So, the view and space you already saw, let me show you the real thing. Food. If you have any questions, please just ask. I can talk about this place forever." - I said and sat down. He nodded and joined me. – "These are several of our specialties we offer on events; please try all of them. In between, I can offer you an ice cream or wine to break the taste."

The table had a variety of several meals: Cesar salad, Summer salad, mini meatballs, Stuffed eggplant with cheese, Chicken apple salad, zucchini chips, different types of quesadillas and two types of soups (French onion soup and tomato soup with parmesan).

"I would gladly accept both, but only if you join me." - he said with a wide smile and placed his folder on the table next to him.

"I will join you for ice cream. So, tell me, how did you find us? What are you looking for in your events?" – I asked as I watched him unpack his folder and take out his laptop.

He placed it between us and opened a presentation with plans and pictures.

"I have actually been here several times already and had brunches as well with partners. That's how we found you. I love your food, but I would love to taste everything you made now. I had a meeting here sitting outside on the terrace, and there was a family next to me. The child was very scared, and out of the blue, you came over with some toys to distract him, and he was quiet again. He forgot about the height of anything that bothered him, and the family offered you a tip, which you refused and told them it's your life job to take care of children. That was the moment I decided I wanted to do business with you and not with your ex-husband." – he said while showing me the slides of the events he wanted to have. It was hard to concentrate, when he said this charming story. In some way, he was charming as well as creepy. I hadn't figured him out yet, but it would be a great business for us according to the presentation. He tried everything we prepared and loved all the food. According to his facial expressions, I made a list of the ones he liked the most and showed him a menu idea, which could fit the events. He really liked it and accepted to work with us and sign the contract as soon as possible.

"My assistant will send you over the documents we need, as well as an event plan, floor plan and menu ideas. We usually do contracts by each event, but as you wish several the whole year, I suggest we make a year contract." – I said and stood up to escort him to the parking.

"Great. Sounds perfect. Once everything is settled, would you be free for a celebratory dinner?" – he asked and handed over a business card. I took it and handed him over mine.

"Sure. We can celebrate. Thank you for coming." – I said, and he nodded and bent in to kiss me on the cheek instead of a handshake. He put his sunglasses on and walked away.

I closed the door and went back to clean up.

"That was weird." – Nate said from the kitchen.

"He was. Who would kiss somebody on the cheek after a business meeting?" – I replied and started to pick up the plates. Nate came over to help me and added.

"Thank God he didn't want me on the meeting. Maybe even I would get a kiss." – we laughed. I don't think so, but I didn't want to ruin his ego. What was the deal with this man? He looked like a gentleman, but there was something else to it.

Within a week, we got the contract ready for a year and all the event dates on the calendar. Zayn was writing to me everyday messages, which were all misunderstanding. He was flirting and also serious, and I couldn't decide where to put this kind of behavior.

Friday was always Lara and Daniel's date night, so I was free to do whatever I wanted. Most of the time, I watched a movie or did some emails that I left during the week. Just as I was about to continue the same routine and make popcorn, I got a message.

Popcorn and movie night?

It was Brian making fun of me or inviting himself over.

As always in my calendar. Today I am watching "The Holiday". Wanna join?

I knew he hated this kind of movie, but I was open to watching something else if I could spend the night with him. I meant watching a movie. Since we had a pregnancy test, our relationship was on a test. We spoke barely, and he was always busy with something and avoided coming over in the evening. He suddenly became a morning person and did breakfast or morning runs with me. Maybe, he changed back to the Brian who loves movies and would come over. Then, I got a message from Zayn.

Send me your address. I will come and pick you up in an hour.

Shit. The dinner. I totally forgot about that. It's business, so I had to do it, but Brian was finally coming around. I hate to disappoint.

Sorry. No movie tonight. Forgot my business dinner. Re-schedule?

As I pressed send, there was a knock on the door. I went over to open it was Brian, who teleported in a second to my front door.

"Hey." – he smiled and showed the bottle of wine he had

with him and a bag of popcorn he made at home.

"Hey. I... I....I am sorry. I feel so stupid now. I just sent you a message I have to cancel." – he came in and placed the wine and popcorn on the kitchen and took out his phone to check his messages.

"No worries. I was already on my way when I wrote you. So, when do you leave? Can I stay and watch a movie? Maybe Lara will join me." - he took off his jacket, and the shirt he had on was so slim that I could see his skin and chest, which took my thoughts somewhere else.

"He is the big startup owner I told you about, with whom we just signed that major contract. He will pick me up in less than an hour. I totally forgot about it. The man is kind of a creep in some way but let's see. It's business anyway." – I opened the bottle of wine and poured Brian a glass. – "Wanna help me with choosing a dress?" – I gave him a smirk and went to the bedroom, where he followed me.

"What did you have in mind?" – He sat on the bed with the wine in his hand and looked like a perfect gay best friend giving fashion advice.

"I think we will go somewhere elegant, something with dark colors. A dress for sure." – I took out a few and threw them on the bed. – "These might work. Let me change, and I can try these on." – I took black bra and matching underpants out and placed them on the bed with thin black stockings.

"Are you sure you are going for a business meeting?" – Brian took my underwear and threw it at me.

"I like nice underwear. Leave me alone. It's a business meeting. I have to be convincing." – I put the pants on my shoulders and strutted to the bathroom.

"You convinced me for sure." - Brian shouted after me.

I threw my comfy home clothes on the floor and changed into my underwear and stocking. When I walked out, Brian almost spilled the wine out and stared at me, speechless.

"Sorry. I will get dressed." – I picked up the first dress and tried it on.

"No, you don't have to. You…you…." – I turned towards the mirror and caught his eyes all over me. I looked away and picked up the first option which was a little black satin dress, with a closed front and an open V-back. I was almost 45 years old, but I was never as fit as now. Dressing up for a man brought me back to my teenage years. I felt young and beautiful. I forgot the wrinkles around my eyes, the skin on my neck, which was losing up and my menopause.

"What do you think?" – I asked, looking at him in the mirror.

"You look beautiful. Maybe try this one." – he handed me another dress, which wasn't this open and more conservative-professional.

"Alright. Let me do my make-up first." I sat down and put eyeliner on and mascara, w and took out a little red lipstick for later. I took off the other dress and put on the new one. Whenever I looked at Brian, he made me blush, and I could only smile. This dress was closed in the front and back as well with a U-neck. It was wider, and I had a perfect reddish belt which suited it perfectly. I try to reach the zip, but it was far away. Brian stood up, placed the glass on the bedside table and came over to help me.

"Let me." – he whispered and slowly started to pull up the zip. He placed one hand on my waist and stayed close to my neck. I could feel every breath he blew out. – "I think this is it."

"I… I…I like it too." – I couldn't take my eyes away from his eyes, and he came closer and gave me a soft, warm kiss on the neck. I closed my eyes and breathed in heavily. – "Brian…I…"

"Tell me to stop, and I will." – he said and continued to kiss my neck. I couldn't move, speak and barely held myself together. The moment was broken by the sound of the doorbell.

"Stop." – I said and ran off to open the door. He was here. What was just happening? I got back to the bedroom. – "I have to go. I am sorry. Thank you and um… what was that?" – I stopped at the door for an answer, but I only got a cheeky grin, and he said.

"Have a nice dinner! I'll clean up here. See you later. Good luck!"

I turned away and ran off to pick up my phone and bag. My legs were shaking from the feeling, and I knew I wanted more than anything to stay there and not let him stop. Why? Why was this happening now?

"Hello. Wow! You look amazing!" – said Zayn, who stood in front of the entrance and caught me by surprise.

"Hello. Thank you! You are not bad yourself." – he smiled back at me.

We went to an elegant restaurant. Zayn didn't let me choose my food, and he ordered everything for me, which was at first a nice touch, but how did he know what I like or what I want? I let him as I didn't want to be impolite. He asked me a lot of questions about my life and Lara. He was interested in everything I had to say and barely let me ask him anything. When I did, his response was more open, and I never knew if he told me the truth or an approximate response. When we finished dinner, instead of driving, we walked to my place. It wasn't that far away, and a bit of fresh air would do me good. When we got to the entrance, it was open, so I turned towards him to say farewell, but he insisted on going up with me.

"There are a lot of bad stories and movies about buildings with open entrance doors. I better make sure you are alright, and I will close it on the way out." – this was his excuse. I found it odd, but I let him be a gentleman.

We took the stairs to the second floor, and I took the keys out to open the door.

"Thank you for the lovely evening. I am glad we made that contract, and thank you for getting me safely to my door." – I bent to give him a kiss on the cheek as the door opened and Lara was standing there.

"Hey, mom. Hello sir. I heard voices and was sure it was you." – she said with a smile and turned away and continued – "I was right it is just mom." – she shouted, and Brian came from the back who saw the man next to me and just smiled and walked away. He was still here.

"This is my daughter, Lara. This is Zayn. He will do some events in the restaurant, and we went out to celebrate." – I added and looked for Brian in the back, but he was gone.

"Nice family. Thank you, Tess, for the evening. I hope to see you soon." – he kissed me on the cheek, and I turned to go inside as Brian was standing in front of me, ready to leave.

"Stay." – I said and placed my hand on his chest to stop him. This time I didn't let him leave without talking to me.

"I can't and shouldn't. I hope your dinner went well. See you, Lara. Don't eat all the popcorn." – he turned to me and put my hand down and walked out. He is bailing out on me and keeping me speechless.

I walked over to Lara and sat next to her on the couch and snuggled into her. She hugged me and handed me over the popcorn. Finally, food I actually wanted to have tonight. We watched another movie together. I felt my body is present, but my mind was thinking about Brian and our recent moments, which were either interrupted or led me to an unknown feeling I didn't know where to put.

The first celebration we had was graduation. Lara had her exams all the way until the day before the graduation ceremony. She was always a good student, and I never had to remind her to concentrate. She was doing it on her own as she had a clear goal in front of her to get into Cornell University. After the ceremony, we went to the restaurant, where Zayn appeared out of the blue and at the end, he joined us at the table. Our table was more like a party than a family table. Steve and his family were here, mom with her husband, Daniel with his family, Nate, Brian and Zayn who nobody knew how he got there as the restaurant was closed, but he brought presents as well. There was an uncomfortable air between Zayn and Brian as was between Zayn and me. He wanted to be always next to me but made me feel weird, so I sent Nate to entertain him. Daniel and Lara had to leave for their party, which Brian offered to take them to. Steve and his family were also leaving, too, as Vincent got into London Business School and applied for a summer course, which he was going to leave for in two days. They wanted to go with him and sort out everything for him to make sure he was in the best place. They rented him an apartment over a skype interview, and all of us were skeptical about it, so they wanted to make sure it was alright. Mom and her husband went with them as well, and Nate and I stayed with Zayn.

"Would you like to come to my place after this?" – he came behind me and whispered to my ear.

"I am sorry. I have to clean up here. Maybe another time." – I smiled and walked away, but he followed.

"Nate can do it, and the staff. Lara is off, what do you have to do? Just a quick drink?" – he said, and I turned to face him and placed an arm on his shoulder to keep him on arm distance.

"I am just busy. We can re-schedule, alright?"

"What if I keep you company?" – he added and took me by the hand.

"Look. I think you got the wrong idea. I liked our dinner, but it's just business. I like you as a business partner, but I do not want anything more." - he still didn't let my arm go and made an angry face. – "Please let me go and leave."

"Everything alright?" – Nate came out of the kitchen as he heard me say it louder. Once he appeared, Zayn let go of my hand and just went out without saying anything. I took my hand, and it was already a bit red and started to hurt as he squeezed it. – "What was that?"

"Can you call somebody and check on this guy? I don't like this. There is something not right about him. How did he know we were here?" – I asked worriedly and took some ice for my hand.

"I'll ask the kitchen staff; they must know somebody, and we can check him out. Are you alright? Would you like me to drive you home?" – He put his arm around me and handed me some ice.

"Can you stay with us until we know? We have to finish Laras' gift anyway." – I turned and finished cleaning up.

We never asked the kitchen staff to clean after us or think they should serve us; we used the restaurant like our own kitchen, and they respected our decision. Nate and I closed up and went home to finish Lara's graduation present. We looked around all the way to see if Zayn followed us, but we didn't see him anywhere. We wanted to surprise Lara for her graduation with a trip to New York, including Daniel, to get her sorted for University. When we asked Daniel, he was first happy but then declined to come. They decided that their last night would be the graduation to close this wonderful chapter until he transferred to New York. They seemed distanced the last months, and I think both he and Lara knew it would not work out and were just preparing for the farewell. Nate and I planned to design the whole flat like a small New York and Cornell University. We ordered all the props months ago from Amazon and stored them in the restaurant to build them up when she came home from the party to surprise her. We even had a small Statue of Liberty, which was in the middle of the living room. The whole flat was just like a small city. Nate and I had fun building it up and laughed a lot. When we finally finished, we just sat on the couch until we heard the door opening. It was not even 11 p.m., and she was back. Her make-up was all over her face; she was crying her soul out. Nate and I jumped up and ran over to her.

"What's wrong? What happened?" – I asked her and hugged her

"We broke up." – she started to cry even harder. They knew it and decided this a long time ago, but it still hurt like hell. It was her first heartbreak, and she was falling into pieces. She just melted on the floor and leaned back on the door cleaning her face from the tears without even looking up. – "I loved him. I knew this would come, but it… it….What is all this?" – then she suddenly realized what was in front of us.

"We wanted to surprise you and build you a small New York as part of your present." – Nate said and kissed her on top of her head.

"I am sorry you have to feel this way, but it might be the best for you to face this now, rather than later when you are in New York." – I joined in the family hug. The three of us sat leaned back to the entrance door and watched the amazing New York city we built without saying anything else. The silence was broken when our nice Statue of Liberty fell from the table and fell into pieces, and we all started to laugh. It was just the perfect ice breaker.

"I love you guys. What's the present, because I can't take all this cardboard with me?" – she asked, looking up at us.

"We are all going to New York with you to help you settle." – I said, and Lara's sadness disappeared, and a new smile came back to her kind face.

"That's so cool, but you know Jake is there as well as is Ramos. Are you okay with that?" – she looked up at me.

"Sure I am. Nate and I will have fun while you do some networking and maybe even let Ramos join us." – I played the cool mom, but I wasn't. I totally and absolutely forgot about Ramos. What if he came with a top model? I hadn't spoken to him in over a year already.

We had two months before we all flew to New York, but before that, we still had my 45th birthday. Lara had bad days when she talked about Daniel and how big a mistake they made, but she also had her good moments when she was happy to have a fresh start. I planned my birthday at home and invited all my friends, colleagues and family over and thanks to a catering company we didn't have to do a single thing other than enjoy ourselves. We had a lot of food, dancing, drinking the whole day. The party started at 2 pm and the last guests left around 10 pm. At the end, the catering company stayed to clean up, until Lara, Nate and Brian joined me in opening the presents. I got so many relaxing bath products from my girlfriends that I started to get worried about what they thought about my stress level. It was some kind of a secret message. I got a ticket to New York for two for Christmas to visit Lara from Steve and Nicole. The second ticket was without a name, so they left me the option to choose with whom I wanted to go with. I got a few kitchen accessories from mom and her husband, which I loved and could never have enough.

"I don't want to be mean, but I don't see any present from you, Nate or Brian. I will make a note of it for the future." – I said, trying to be mean.

"I promised to tell you my opinion when you are 45 if you don't know it by now." – Nate said, and Brian and I looked confused. Lara seemed to know as she smiled.

"Nate, that was a long time ago." – I said and started to put the presents back.

"Actually, I don't have to say anything." – he looked over to Lara, who stood up and ran off.

"Did I miss a family meeting, what are you talking about?" – I asked suspiciously.

"Come mate, let me drive you home and leave these two ladies." – Nate stood up and tapped Brians' shoulder, who was as confused as I was.

"Alright. Mystery it is then." – Brian added and started to get dressed when he saw Lara exit the room with a letter in her hand. A letter he recognized and looked at Nate, who only smiled.

"I promised her, and I will keep this promise. She has to know. Sorry man." – Nate added, but Brian just took off and shut the door. – "Wait up." – Nate ran after him, and they were gone.

"What was that about?" – I asked Lara, but she only handed me the letter. – "What's this?" – I took it from her hands

"You remember when we had a farewell party for Brian when he moved out a long time ago?" – Lara started

"Yes." – it was so long ago that I almost forgot. It was over ten years ago. Who would remember everything from that day? – "Yeah, we made the picture for him, right?"

"Yes. Do you also remember he was gone for a while in the middle of the party?" - I nodded. It was quite blurry, but I remember he went away, and Lara went after him, but I thought they were in the bathroom.

"He wrote a letter then. This letter, actually. He gave it to me and told me to hold onto it until I leave. When I leave, and you are still single, I should give it to you. I was skeptical about that Zayn man, but dad told me he was a creep and nothing more. So here I am. This is our present for you. Truth." – I looked down the envelope, and it was closed and never opened. How could she keep something like this for so long?

The Vow

"Do you know what's in it?" – I asked and started to open it.

"I don't, but I know that when Brian was having a shower, something happened, and I hope with this letter you will find your way back to each other. You have been friends for over 30 years. It's worth fighting for. I miss the time you were hanging out more." – she stood up, went out and left me to read it in peace.

Dearest Tess,

I hope you will have the chance to read this message. We spent the last three years living together with a small devil I loved the first moment I saw her in the hospital all those years ago. The first night in your apartment, you made me feel welcomed with your movie nights and hot cocoa. I then realized all the things I have missed out on by having only one-night stands and never actually being with someone to build this kind of relationship with. The trust, fun and love you two have for each other is something one can only wish for. The warmth of the apartment was reflecting everything you have in your heart locked away. You got your heart broken into pieces once, and it will be hard to open that lock and give someone a chance, but I hope you will. When we were silly kids, we promised to marry each other if we were single and didn't want to be alone. I could never imagine a marriage

159

out of force like that, but out of love? Yes. We had our chances, and we decided to stay friends over and over. We put our friendship first and would give everything up for each other. Not only for you but for Lara as well. When you asked me to be her godfather, I wanted to be her friend more than anything. A person she would maybe tell a secret to before you. Someone she could trust and a person who will be there for her when a boy breaks her heart. I would punch the guy for sure. I would never want to replace Nate's part in her life as a father. That's not the only person I want to be. There will come a moment when the little bird will leave the nest, and the mama bird stays behind. I want to be the other bird keeping her company, giving her love and all she deserves. I realized this now, and who knows what I might be like in 15 years, but one thing will be sure. I will love you always. If you give me a chance to show you, I am not that heartbreaking, one-night stand type who will break you and leave you, I promise you I will make you happy. You will wake up with a coffee on your bedside table every day, I will clean and behave, I would gladly spend every hour you wish in the restaurant or with whomever and wherever you want. At night I promise I will touch you and show you my love as much as possible and will hold you forever. We will grow old together and get fat from all the hot cocoa. We will see Lara walk down the aisle and be proud of the person she becomes. Whatever our lives bring us. I will wait for you as you are worth it. This I promise you. I gave Lara this letter, as I know she knows you better than anyone to know the right time. I can only wish I will be there to see it.

Love,

Brian

CHAPTER 7

I didn't read the letter once, twice, but at least four times, and I sobbed each time. My dress was wet from all the tears. After all these years, why now? How could Nate and Lara keep this from me for so long? I spent days and nights crying about this person. He treated me several times like he didn't care. When we finally got together on one of my drunk nights, he left. I still didn't understand that. I jumped up and took my phone. I need to call Nate.

"Why didn't he speak to me and ignored me after something actually happened? Tell me. I am lost." – I asked without waiting for Nate to say anything.

"Sometimes, you can be really stupid, Tess. You told Lara it would never happen and made him feel as though you were ashamed of it. Lara knew what happened the whole time and was happy for you to find that love again, but each time you opened your mouth and wanted to "protect" her, you hurt him and pushed him away. I never liked him, you know that, but he truly put you first every time and would always do that." - Nate paused, then continued – "You know what you have to do, Tess. Don't talk to me, call him." – he hung up.

I never thought I would say this, but he was right. I hurt him back with all the comments and made him feel that way because he did the same when we were young. I was a stupid teenager behaving like a fool and living in the past. I loved him always, I just never wanted to accept the fact it could be something more. What am I waiting for? I picked up the phone and dialed Brian, who picked up faster than I thought.

"Tess. I am …." – he started then stopped.

"Me too. Can we meet up? I want to see you." – I smiled but then was interrupted by a doorbell. There was always somebody coming to this place at the wrong time. – "Wait, somebody is at the door. Can you hold?"

"Yeah, sure." – he replied.

I put the phone down and opened the door without looking with a huge smile on my face, which disappeared when I saw who it was.

"What are you doing here?" – I demanded.

"Happy Birthday. I assumed my invitation got lost." – Zayn said.

"Tess? Are you alright? I am coming over." – said Brian

loudly, but before I could say anything, Zayn grabbed the phone from my hand.

"She is alright. Bye." – Zayn said and hung up.

"What are you doing here? Please leave and give me my phone back." – I said confidently, but inside I was freaking out. Zayn threw my phone on the floor, away from my reach and stalked towards me. He closed the door behind him with a huge grin.

"I am here to celebrate your birthday with you. I have champagne for us and thought we could have some cake as well if there is anything left." – he let himself in and started to take out glasses from the kitchen. The only luck I had was that the catering company was still on the terrace, and it made me feel a bit secure. Instead of going after him, I went towards my phone, but then he looked at me angrily and said – "I don't think that's a good idea. Come and have a drink with me."

I changed the direction and went slowly over to the kitchen. I was frightened and scared as hell.

"Why are you here and somehow always everywhere? Are you stalking me?" – I asked and sat on the barstool near the kitchen counter.

"I knew the first moment I saw you that we are made for each other. So, I am here for you, love." – he responded in a calm voice.

"I don't think so. I told you that this is a mistake. I don't feel that way about you. I want to help you with your event, but I will have to cancel if this continues." – he walked over and handed me the champagne glass but still was standing an arms distance away from me. – "I want you to leave, Zayn. Please. Lara can be home any minute." – I begged him, but he didn't move.

"I won't hurt you, Tess. I just love you and want to be with you. Is that a problem… to love somebody? Let's have a toast and enjoy our peace alone. Shall we?" – he raised his glass for a toast. He didn't know the catering team is still outside. They were indeed extremely quiet, but they were my only chance to get out of here. I had to get away somehow. I smiled and raised my glass and poured it all over his face.

"What are you doing?" – he shouted and closed his eyes to wash the burning feeling of champagne in eyes while I jumped up from the stool, threw my glass on the floor and ran out to the terrace while screaming for help. Zayn was close after me, who caught my hand just as I was about to reach the terrace.

"Where are you going, Tess?" – he shouted and looked angry, but then saw all the staff behind me and slowly let go of my arm and made a smile. - "I see you have company."

"Is everything alright, Tess?" - one of the waiters asked me.

"Please call the police, John. Now." – I shouted and started walking back to the staff who stood around me.

Zayn turned and ran out like a rat to his hole. Without closing the door, he was gone. John called the police and gave me a glass of water to calm down. I was shaking and could barely move.

"John can you bring me my phone please?" – he went in for it. I was breathing hard; my hands were shaking, and tears were running down my cheeks. Thank God Lara wasn't at home. What a psychopath. I had to call Brian back; he must have been so worried. As soon as John brought me my phone, I saw several missed calls from him. I called him a few times, but it went to voicemail. Where was he? He said he was on his way before Zayn took the phone. He would be here already, even with big traffic. I called Nate, and he picked up the phone.

"Nate? Zayn was here. He is dangerous. Please call Lara as soon as possible to know where she is. I called the police already."

"Lara is fine. She is with me. What happened? Are you alright? Did he hurt you?" – he asked, sounding incredibly worried.

"Still shaking a bit, but I am fine. I was on the phone with Brian when he came over. He took my phone, and I couldn't call for help. The catering team was thankfully here, otherwise, I don't know what could have happened." – I took a sip of the water, then continued. – "I tried calling Brian, but he isn't picking up. Can you try as well?"

"Yeah, sure. We are coming to your place. Stay still and relax." – he hung up.

I sat for a few minutes on the terrace. When the catering team was ready, all of them came over to double-check if I was alright and asked many times if they should stay, but I let them leave. Lara and Nate came home just as the catering team left. Both of them were worried when they saw me sitting outside looking at the view. I looked pale and as my thoughts left my mind for a few minutes.

"I was so worried, mom. Are you ok?" – Lara sat next to me and hugged me.

"I am alright. Did you get Brian? I am worried." – I looked up at Nate, who shook his head.

It was getting too cold to be outside, so we went in, and I made tea for us, but mostly for me to calm down. I was still thinking about Brian and calling him all the time. There was something wrong; I knew it. It was almost midnight when I got a call from an unknown number. I was looking at the phone and skeptical if I should pick it up or not, but then I did.

"Hello?" – I said.

"Hello, Madam. I am Steve Marshall from the Police Department. Am I speaking to Tess?" – a man said

"Yes, this is she. Did you get him? Are we safe?" – I asked, and both Nate and Lara looked at me with hope in their eyes.

"Mam, I am not sure we are speaking about the same thing."

"The man Mr. Marshall. Zayn something, who attacked me in my home. We called it in a few hours ago. He is a psychopath and a stalker. Did you get him?" – my voice was shaking. I wanted that bastard to get caught.

"I am sorry Mam'. We are not calling in regards of that." – he paused then continued. – "There has been an accident. You were the last caller. Do you know a Brian Shepard?"

"What? What? I don't understand. What accident? Is he alright? Where is he?" – I started crying.

"He had a car accident. It's most possible he won't survive. We wanted to let you know he is in the St. Stevens Hospital. We are sorry. The doctors are doing their best."

I dropped the phone and collapsed. Nate took the phone and finished the call. I couldn't hear anything anymore. I was broken. Is it possible that when I finally could get my happy ending, it is falling into pieces? After years, we admit our feelings, and we got our chance to be together, and it is all over. He was gone. The man I wanted to share my life with was gone.

CHAPTER 8

How does it feel to not have the chance to tell someone you love them? Terrible, unexplainable and something you would never understand until you are in that situation. My subconscious was eating me up. It was all my fault. Everything was my fault. If I hadn't called him, he would have never been in an accident. Every night I fell asleep crying and blaming myself. I couldn't have saved him. I was praying to get one more chance to see him and tell him everything. I flew back to the years of loss, when I lost my stepdad or my grandparents. It was like somebody ripped my heart out. It took me so much time to find it and bring myself back to life. To find the joy and the reason to wake up. Lara was the light at the end of the tunnel and the reason for me to live.

Now we were already on the plane to New York and helping her move away. She was sleeping next to me, as was Nate. I was staring out of the window and looking for a sign that my life would be alright. When we landed, I wanted to go to catch a cab, but Lara said she arranged everything already and I don't have to worry. She even booked us a hotel, which I was not interested in. I wanted to know she was safe and in a good place. We were just about to leave the airport when I saw a man holding a sign with Lara and heart next to it. He was tall and muscular, but not too much, just the type who simply takes care of himself. His charming smile and bright eyes were the only thing I could recognize. It was Jake. He was so handsome, like his dad, just a younger version of him. His tanned skin was simply so smooth. Lara ran over and jumped on him and kissed him all over the face like when they were kids. I spoke to Jake on the phone but didn't see him for years. The small boy who left the apartment many years ago became a grown-up man.

"Jakey. You are so handsome" – I hugged him strongly, and he hugged me back.

"I missed you, Tess." – he said and reached out for Nate to come for a hug.

"I missed you too." – said the voice behind us. We turned to see who it was, and it made my heart jump a bit.

"Hey Ramos." – I went over to hug him, and at that moment, I could just cry. I missed him so much, I wanted to tell him everything that happened. He held me tight and close to him like the last time we hugged and never wanted to let go.

Ramos took my bags, and Jake took Lara's, and we went outside to the car, which was a huge limousine. We stopped and were shocked to see such luxury in one of the World's most expensive cities.

"We are going to drop your things in the hotel, then to their flat, and we can check out the University in the afternoon." – said Ramos as we sat in the car. The hotel was luxurious, with a huge golden lobby. I assumed we would be more than shocked to see the bill. When we got in, Nate and I went to the check-in desk. The reception desk was made out of marble, and there were two receptionists behind it, looking at the guests with a kind smile on their faces. The concierge already waved the bellboy to prepare our bags to be brought to our rooms.

"Welcome to the Grand Cornell Hotel. Do you have a room reservation?" – said the kind lady.

"Yes. Here are our passports and credit card." – I handed everything over, and she started typing, then handed it back.

"Thank you. Mr. Garcia already settled the bill for you in advance. He wanted to make sure you have a good room, so we gave you an upgrade to our Luxury Suite, with two bedrooms and a view over the lake. Your room is on the

6th floor, but my colleague will show you the way. All the bags will be delivered to the room in a few minutes. Anything else I can do you for you?"

"Thank you very much." – we took the keys, and I went over to Ramos. – "Why did you pay? You shouldn't have but thank you very much."

He bent down and kissed me on the cheek.

"You have been through enough, Tess. Just let me give you something. Plus, I don't think you wanted to share a bed with Nate again." – we both laughed, and I smiled gratefully.

We didn't even go up to the room but rather left to see the flat where Jake and Tess would live. As Jake was planning to stay in New York and got a full scholarship, he used the money Ramos planned for studies to buy a small flat close to the university with two bedrooms. The only costs they had were utilities, which I insisted were to be paid by us.

On the ride over to the flat, we were all looking out the windows and exploring the area. It was different in Manhattan and the busy streets in the center. It was more local and fuller with students. There were several universities, one next to each other. The grand library was just around the corner, as was the university. The flat was in a building on the main road, but it was on the 9th floor, so you couldn't hear anything from the streets. When we got in, it still smelled like fresh paint.

"We just finished all the works a few days ago. I hope you like it." – Jake opened the door, and we were all amazed by the flat. It was a grey, green design with a lot of modern furniture. When you entered, the living room and kitchen had a nice bar part, which was set up as a dining area. On the right side of the entrance was a small guest bathroom. At the end of the living room, just opposite the entrance, were two sliding doors for each of the bedrooms, with an ensuite bathroom and a wardrobe. Jake's room was dark blue with a grey combination, and he designed Laras' room with pink and white. He paid attention to each detail in her room to make it homey and similar to her room at home. There were pictures of us all everywhere. Nate, Jake and Lara were in the kitchen talking, and I went to look around the flat. I stopped at the pictures in Laras' room and saw a picture of Brian, Lara and me when he moved out. I took the picture in my hand, and tears were dropping. I held it close to my heart and stood there for a while with closed eyes.

"I am sorry, Tess." – Ramos said when he entered the

room.

"Thank you. It will be alright, I am sure." – I put back the picture and continued my sightseeing. – "The flat is amazing. Very homey."

"Yeah. Jake loved your flat and wanted to make it similar. Ever since we moved away, he was repeating to me how much he loved to be there." – he said and came after me. – "I loved it too. I missed you really." – he took me by the hand and turned me towards him.

"I missed you too, Ramos, but we are worlds apart now. Come, let's go back to the kids." – I took my hand away and walked back to the kitchen while cleaning my tears away.

We spent the next week exploring the city, the best restaurants, cooking in the flat all together and enjoying our time together. We even had a pajama party in the flat when all of us slept together. Jake and Lara were closer and closer every day. They were more like a boyfriend and girlfriend than friends. The last night, we went to a Michelin restaurant downtown. We had an early flight to catch, and we didn't want Lara to come with us to the airport. It would make it harder to say goodbye. After dinner, we walked back to their flat, and it was time. Nate and I hugged Lara as hard as possible and didn't want to let her go. I promised her I won't cry, but hell, I couldn't keep it back. I was sobbing, as was she.

"I will miss you, mom. Call me anytime. I am here for you." – she whispered into my ear

"I love you too darling. Always. You will achieve great things. I am proud of you. My door is always open for you." – I cupped her face and kissed her on her forehead.

"I love you too. We are very proud of you." – Nate added and took my hand to slowly start walking away. I hugged Nate around his waist and cried to him all the way until we got back.

"Thank you for being there for me. I love you." – I told him, and he placed his head on mine and held me close around my waist.

"I got you. It will be alright. We all are."

When we got back to the hotel, Ramos was waiting in the lobby for us.

"May I speak to you?" – he asked me, and I nodded and left Nate to go back to our room.

We sat down in the hotel bar for a drink. I needed

something more than ever.

"I was wondering if you would be alright if I was around more." – he spilled it out once we sat down and placed his hand on mine.

"I am sorry?" – I asked, confused

"I will be working from New York for the next few weeks, and as the company and my work are done here, I would be moving back. I would really like to catch up with you and take you out if you would give me a chance." –It was so tempting, but it wasn't the right time.

"I would be happy to have you around, but please give me time." – he nodded and agreed. We drank and talked about everything that happened the past few years. He told me about the girls he dated and about the woman I saw when I stopped talking to him. He laughed about the story about Zayn, but I was more freaked out and kicked him under the table a few times. He wanted to ask about Brian, but I could feel my voice shaking whenever he or I mentioned his name. I wasn't ready yet to talk about it.

When we returned home, I spent a few nights sleeping in Lara's room and hugging her pillow and breathing in her smell. I missed her so much. My life felt so empty, and it was hard for me to enjoy anything outside of being in the restaurant. The first two months we talked every day, she wrote to me or called me to tell me everything and to check on me, but then she started to get busier, and instead of FaceTime, it was mostly audio calls, where I could hear giggling in the back with Jake. I was happy to hear her voice, even without seeing her and knowing she was doing well. Ramos was moving back, and I offered to pick him up from the airport. As his flat was rented out ever since they left and the lease was going to expire in a month, I offered him to stay in the guest bedroom. He wanted to stay in a hotel and not be in my way, but I insisted; it was the least I could do for him after everything he gave Lara. Plus, I wanted some company. I was very lonely and lost my will to go out see friends or family. Every time somebody called me, I felt like a patient, and they called to see if I had killed myself. I felt a bit disappointed they thought of how weak I was. I have been through so much already in my life. I just needed time and space.

The month with Ramos was a lot of fun. We found ourselves continuing where we left off. Not in a romantic way, but he was my rock once again. We shared our days with each other, had nice dinners together on the terrace or in front of the TV. We had FaceTime calls with the children together, and it felt like the old days. One night, when Lara and Jake called, they asked about Christmas and if we were coming over, and I got several extra calls on my phone, which I postponed, but then decided to pick up.

"Sorry, sweetheart. Let me pick this up, it could be important." – I stood up from the couch and went to pick up the phone.

"Hello?"

"I am calling you from the St. Stevens Hospital. We have good news for you. Brian is awake." – I turned and just hung up the phone and froze. I felt my heart which was frozen for so long, finally start beating again.

"Everything alright?" – asked Lara as Ramos looked at me worried.

"Tess?" – Ramos added

"He is awake. I have to go. I am sorry. I will call you later." – I added and picked my bag and coat and ran out before they could say anything. I ran to my car and drove to the hospital. I ran to the room, which I visited almost every day to bring some flowers or talk a bit. I was running down the corridor when I stopped just a few steps before the door and slowly walked to the entrance.

"Tess?" – his weak voice said and turned his face towards me. I dropped my bag and coat on the chair just right next to the door, went over to the bed, kneeled next to him, and held his hand with glassy eyes.

"I am here. I am here." – I repeated while placing my head on his bed next to his hands.

"They said I was in an accident. What happened?" – he looked at me confused and still tired. All the scars were almost gone from his face, his broken leg and arm were already in good condition. His main scar on his head was healing slower, but it was barely visible next to his hair.

"I called you to come over when I read your letter. Zayn, the psychopath, followed me and attacked me, and you got distracted while driving trying to call me back. You went through a red light and got hit by a truck. You were in a coma for 5 months, Brian." – his face was as shocked as mine was to see him. I thought I had lost him forever. – "When the police called, they said they wouldn't be able to save you. Your heart stopped beating, and you had no pulse. When they brought you into the hospital, they saved you, but you were already half gone. Every time I came to visit you, the nurses gave me hope to keep coming."

"I heard your voice. It was like a dream. It was something about Lara and New York. I am sorry." – he took my face with his hand and held my chin while smiling at me. I stood up and sat on the bed next to him.

"I thought I lost you." – tears were piling up in my eyes when I looked at him.

"I will never leave you." – he closed his eyes and fell asleep with a smile. The nurse came in and asked me to leave him to rest. I went over to the doctor to ask him about his condition.

"Will he be alright?"

"It's a miracle he is awake. He will be fine. All his results are good. He needs to relax a bit and get physiotherapy to get walking back and gain a bit of muscle. He can leave the hospital in a week." – he smiled at me and tapped me on the shoulder and left me.

He will be fine. I texted Nate and Ramos about the news and called Lara to tell her.

"How is he?" - she picked up the phone in a hectic manner.

"He will be out in a week. He is doing fine." – the tears I

gathered in my eyes were sliding my face, and I walked to my car slowly.

"I am so happy, mom. See, there is plenty of good news to come. Will he be able to come for Christmas with you?"

"It's a month away. I don't know, honey; he just woke up. I am just happy he is alive at all. Let's see how everything goes." – my phone started to ring once again with an unknown number again. – "Honey, I have another call. Let's talk later. Don't worry, alright?"

"Sure, mom. Love you." – she hanged up, and I picked up the other caller.

"This is the police department, Steve Marshall speaking. How are you doing, mam'? We heard the great news today" – said the kind policeman, who called me about Brian and was my main contact in the search for Zayn, who disappeared months ago.

"Thank you, officer. I hope you have some other good news for me." - I asked as I sat in my car.

"Yes, indeed. We found him. He was hiding in a luxury house in Cuba. They are probably just out there taking him into custody. We found other women who were the victims of his assault, and some even had mental issues after that and finished in hospitals. You were lucky. I wish you a lovely day, Tess. I hope your luck continues."

I put the phone down and placed my head back into the seat and closed my eyes. Finally, my life was coming back to normal. From happiness or relief, I suddenly started laughing. It was all going to be alright.

When I got home from the hospital, I told Ramos about everything. He seemed sad to lose me to another man in moments, but it was clear to him the moment he moved in, my heart belonged to someone else. As much as he tried, he wanted to be part of my life more than ever; it wasn't necessarily a romantic way, but a person on whom I could count on. We had our romance, but it wasn't the end game. I gained a valuable friend, but the person I wanted to grow old with was someone else. Ramos offered to help change the flat to a more comfortable one and buy some things to train with Brian at home to get his muscles back. He was quite fit and knew his way how to start from scratch to get your body back. He offered to come every day and do work outs with him and help me with the shower. That was the hardest as he was still unstable to walk, and I had to help him get in and out. While Ramos and I helped Brian, Nate offered to take care of the restaurant. Brian was back in my guest bedroom and sleeping like a baby for long hours. Ever since he left the hospital and lived with me, our days were mostly about getting him better. Ramos was coming every day in the morning, and in the evenings, we went for short walks around the block. It was a reason to get out and get some fresh air. Whenever one of us started the conversation about us, we were interrupted by a call or somebody coming over. We left it as it is and only shared brief touches and smiles. I was happy he just was alive.

It was a week before Christmas when I wanted to see if Brian could make it to New York. I drove to the restaurant for the last check before we left and to check everything was ok. The whole team was super prepared, and Nate handled all issues professionally, as always. When I got home, the flat was all in the dark, and there were only some candles lit up, but I could barely see anything. Until Brian came out behind the kitchen wall, holding a bouquet of roses and a candle in another hand.

"What is all this?" – I asked silently while placing all my stuff on the floor and started walking towards him.

"We never had the time to really talk. I asked everybody who interrupted us to leave us at least two hours to ourselves." – he handed the flowers over to me, and I took them and breathed in the fresh smell of fresh roses.

"They are gorgeous. Thank you." – I placed them on the kitchen table and turned back to him. – "Why two hours?"

"I will give you fifteen minutes to finish your thoughts about the letter you never had the chance, and then I would like to kiss you for the rest." – He put his arms around my waist and pulled me close, looking deep into my eyes.

"I… I…I can't really concentrate like this. You make me nervous." – I looked down, but he took my chin and pulled me back and kissed me once, then twice softly.

"How about now?" – he whispered to my mouth.

"I love you too." – I kissed him back and put my arms around his neck, and pulled him in. It was the longest kiss we had ever had. We didn't want to let go. He started to move me towards the bedroom, and I followed his steps but then stopped and looked at him. – "I don't want to hurt you."

"You give me power. I am in perfect shape." – he picked me up into his arms and placed me on the bed. I stared into his glazing eyes and pulled him on top of me. Even if he would be in pain, he would hide it from me and show me he could do it.

"Tess. I am sorry I did this to you." – he added.

"Just shut and kiss me." – we smirked at each other, and he followed the orders. From my mouth, he moved down to my neck from one side to the other, and as he moved down, he unbuttoned my shirt and started to undress me. I was breathing louder and louder, and everything that happened in the past months was forgotten. Our bodies were moving together, enjoying finally being one. We simply didn't want it to end.

"I love you, Tess" – Brian looked over at me while I was staring at the ceiling, searching for my breath. I turned towards him and rolled over to lie on him. I kissed him first on one cheek, then the other, and then his soft, warm mouth.

"I think this answers my part as well." - I didn't need to say anything else. This night was ours. We didn't only have two hours, but the whole evening. We talked about the past all the stupidness we did as teenagers and compared Lara to us. We even thought about Jake and Lara becoming a thing but then just laughed about it. What if?

Two days before Christmas, Nate, Ramos, Brian and I flew

over to New York, where Lara and Jake were waiting for us with a sign, "Three Musketeers". If anyone actually knows the story from Alexandre Dumas, at the end, it was not three, but four musketeers. We booked the same hotel we had last time. It was beautiful, had a great view and food, and was close to the flat. On Christmas Eve, Jake and Lara were cooking for all of us. When we got there, all of us noticed the change in the flat. There was a woman's touch, the kitchen had so much equipment like our kitchen in the restaurant. The bedroom doors were closed and I wondered whether they were hiding a big mess.

When all of us sat at the table, I wasn't able to hold myself back, so I dropped the question.

"What are you hiding in the bedrooms? You never have them closed." – All eyes went to Lara and Jake, who were just about to place the food on the table. They exchanged a look, and Lara was the first to respond.

"Well….we wanted to leave it for later, but if you are so curious, we kind of moved to one place." – she smiled at Jake, and he placed his arm around her waist. We all knew what that meant.

"Oh, Wow. I think none of us were expecting this. How? When?" – Nate said as he laid back in his chair, totally

187

shocked.

"Well, at first it was just roommates, but then like a month after, we kind of got drunk at a party, and we kissed in a university game out of fun, and then….um…." – Lara started the story while taking a seat.

"Then Lara realized what a good kisser I am and couldn't stop." - Jake teased, and Ramos looked proudly at him.

"I am really happy for you. You were somehow always meant to be." - I added. I was truly happy.

CHAPTER 9

The past 25 years with Lara have gone by in the blink of an eye. I can't believe she has grown up so fast. It seems like yesterday she started to walk, not even to think about her first graduation from high school, then the second one from Cornell University. Today is an even bigger moment. As I sit in front of the mirror, one woman doing my makeup, the other my hair, I can barely see what is happening around me. One thing is sure, I am more excited than ever. I am holding onto the arm of the chair and starting to sweat even more. In addition to menopause, excitement and a warm summer day are the worst combinations. When the ladies are done, it is time to do some photos. The photographer is doing so many pictures, you can barely move or do something without any instruction.

"Tess, go closer to Lara. Now smile and make a proud face. Alright, please, ladies, get dressed." – says the photographer, showing the bridesmaids the direction to move from one side of the room to the other.

"She seriously needs a chill pill." – I whisper to Lara. She laughs.

189

"She is super scary." – she whispers back.

Within half an hour, we are all dressed up. It is time for another photo shoot, which nobody enjoys. We have to drink more to get over it, but it's only a few more minutes, and we can go. We still have two hours until the guests come, so I use the time to go get out of crowd and think and breath in some fresh air. If I smoked, it would be the perfect moment to take at least two.

The wedding is in the restaurant, but there is an additional tent built for the ceremony, should it be a rainy day. There are over 150 guests arriving from all over the world. As I sit on the terrace, I see Nate moving left and right and giving directions to the kitchen staff. His new girlfriend, who I haven't met yet, is already here helping him. I see some other guests arriving as well and shaking hands with Nate. Suddenly I feel a touch on my back and turn.

"Are you alright?" – Lara joins me.

"Of course. Just too many people. I needed some fresh air. Too much excitement. How are you?"

"Can't wait. You know I love weddings, even though this is a bit different. I see dad is reorganizing everything." – she says and looks over at the guests.

"Yeah, worst idea to put him in charge of food. What a control freak."

"Says who..." – she pauses – "Come, let's go. We should start soon." – she holds her hand out, and I join her.

The two hours of waiting pass by faster than anything. The whole wedding is usually over in a second, and all you remember after is the pictures and a lot of drinks. We all go down to join the groomsman. We stand behind closed doors and wait for the sign to make the big entrance.

"Nervous?" – asks Ramos, holding me and walking me down the aisle.

"Aren't you?"

"Just go with the flow. It's going to be wonderful." – he bent down and kisses me on the side.

From the darkness of standing inside, the bright light of the sun hits us, blinding us momentarily. Jessie and Vincent, Steves' children, are in front of us as maid of honor and best man. After them, Ramos and I walk, following the rhythm of the music. The guests start to scream and clap. When we reach the end of the aisle Jessie and I go to the left side and Vincent and Ramos to the right. As we turn, there she is. The most beautiful bride I have ever seen. Lara, my baby who walks down the aisle with so much confidence, compared to Nate who is holding her and looking like he is going to faint any second. I turn to the groom, who has tears in his eyes.

Nate turns Lara and gives her a kiss and big hug before handing his daughter to her future husband, Jake.

Jake and Lara agreed not to say any vows but write them and put them in a helium balloon, which they let go. We will never know what they promised each other, but without waiting to say it, Jake kisses the bride.

The party continues with pictures, dancing, eating and the rest, which belongs to a normal wedding day. After the long day, I have my moment in Laras' room, where I go down memory lane, up to the moment Jake and Lara started to date. We never thought that 5 years later, Jake would propose and today we will be at their wedding. It seemed so far away, but here we are. I turn off the light in her room and close the door to her childhood. She is grown up, a wife and soon even a mother, but let's not run ahead too much. She still has time and shouldn't announce it on her honeymoon. She learned from my past how to announce it and that timing is everything. I turn off the light in the living room and kitchen, and as I walk into the bedroom, I see my future.

"Hey there. You looked beautiful today." – he says.

"Thank you. Let me get cleaned up, and I will join you in a bit." – I go to the bathroom to wash off a million layers of makeup and have a refreshing shower. I need five pads to take all the makeup off. Just as I finish, I look in the mirror. I look at my body. I am over fifty now, and I won't get any younger. Every day there are more and more wrinkles around my eyes. The skin on my neck is becoming loose. The silky skin and smoothness are gone. What do you want, Tess? I ask myself every day. I have the man I always wanted; my daughter is happy and married. We are all healthy and happy. Is this how it was supposed to be? Is this my happily ever after? I smile, take out a bobby pin and bend it into the shape of a ring.

"Hey, you." – I say as I come out the bathroom and see Brian sitting in bed reading something on his Kindle with his glasses on. He places it on the bedside table and looks at me with so much love.

"Come here, you soon-to-be grandma." – He says and reaches out for my arms and pushes me to the bed next to him.

"Hey. No no. Let's not rush into things, alright?" – I say and sit on the bed next to him.

"Why do you look like a professor preparing to give me a lesson?"

"I have something to say."

"What's up, Professor?"

"Many, many years ago, you made me a promise; it was not just a simple promise, but to give up everything to be there for me. You showed me loyalty and friendship, which not a lot of people have. You were my rock and were always there for me. You proved yourself to love me many times. There are some things I will never be able to give you back. The day you had your accident, I thought I would never have the chance with you or to tell you how much I love you. I want to tell you now. I love you, Brian. I will always be there for you and will never let you go again. I promise you to be a good partner and to give you all the warmth I have. I will be your partner in crime as well as in bed. I hope to share your dreams." – I stop and take the bobby pin ring out of my pocket. – "So, I kind of made you this ring out of a bobby pin and wanted to ask you if you…."

Without finishing, he jumps at me, kissing me with full power and emotion.

"I never believed you wanted to get married again, but it's a definite yes." – he answers, taking the bobby pin and placing it on his finger. He looks at it and turns it towards me to show me how nice it looks.

"I didn't plan to do a wedding. What about you and me in Bali?" – I ask.

"Deal. You already wrote your vows." – we laugh.

"You made me a promise; I told you my vow."

EPILOGUE

Tess and Brian decided to take a trip to Bali only the two of them to get married under romantic circumstances without making a big celebration and party out of it. A few days before their trip Ramos came over for dinner. On his way to the bathroom, he saw on the kitchen counter a brochure about wedding in the wonderful Intercontinental Bali. Without saying anything he took a picture of it and sent to Lara and Jake to investigate if they would be getting married in Bali without telling the family. Lara was not informed about it, but instead of challenging her mother, she wished her a nice trip and fun. Tess and Brian had a long flight with a stop in Taipei it took them over 20 hours to get to the dream destination. When they checked in, they wanted to confirm everything for the wedding which would be in a week. The concierge had all the correct information, and they were settled to enjoy a week to themselves as boyfriend and girlfriend until they say the big YES in front of a Balinese priest.

The week passed by with exploring the island and finding romantic spots all over the place to enjoy themselves. When the big day came, Tess and Brian were getting ready in traditional Balinese clothes to respect their culture and also to do something unusual. When they went to the beach to join the priest the reception staff was waiting for them with flowers in their hands. The general manager came to speak to them and said.

"Congratulations Mr. and soon to be Mrs. Shepard. We are honored to be part of your wedding day. Before we get start, we wanted to let you know that according to the Balinese culture you have to have at least two witnesses per person. Do you have yours here? – he asked.

Both Brain and Tess looked confused, as nobody informed them about this in advance.

"I am sorry, but we were not informed about this information. Can somebody from the reception join us?" – Tess looked behind the manager for some hope and support from the staff, but nobody said anything.

"May I have a suggestion?" – The manager put his face in front of Tess who started to look depressed and miserable.

"Yes, please do." – Brian added and held Tess's hand to calm her down.

"As part of the tradition, we usually offer family members to be witnesses and part of this great experience." – he said with a kind smile on his face

"That's not going to work, as it is only the two of us." – Tess replied.

"Are you sure?" – the manager said and the staff behind him moved away where the whole family was standing - Lara, Jake, Ramos, Nate, Sasha, Steve, Nicole, Vincent, Jessie, Mom and her husband. They were all here to be part of the big day.

"What are you doing? How did you know?" - Tess asked while almost starting to cry, but instead she could only smile and laugh from surprise.

"You know mom, we are always informed and have eyes and ears everywhere." – Lara added and came to hug them both.

"Did you say something again?" – Tess looked at Brian.

"Wasn't me." – he protected himself and greeted the rest of the family.

"Ramos saw the ad on your kitchen table, and he sent it to us and we did a bit of research and calls to inform us when to join you. We also prepared you a honeymoon, so you are continuing your trip for additional two weeks to

Australia." – Lara said and handed over an envelope with all the details.

"You are insane. This is all insane. I can't believe this is happening." - Tess said and put her hands on her face. It was an unforgettable experience and such a shock at ones.

The wedding started and the couple had a huge smile on their faces. Even though they planned it to do it in secret, they had their family with them to be part of this day. They took a few glances at them and all of them had tears in their eyes. It would have been wrong to not be together. In a family like this where you love each other so much, you would travel not only 20 hours to be there, but also to another planet just to be with each other when the other one needs you. This the actually promise – love one another.

ABOUT THE AUTHOR

"The Vow" is the second part of the "Journey with Tess" series. The first part, "The Promise" was published in October, 2020. The first book reflects the young age of the main character, while "The Vow" was more about adulthood, obligations and starting life after your children leave you. The love for the characters grew as time passed by. They became part of my life as well, and I sometimes even meet people so similar I automatically thought about the characters in the book.

When "The Vow" finished I didn't want to let go of all the people I created. It was a great experience and also a nice challenge to start writing and using the imagination to create stories.

Thank you again to my brother and mother, who read the books several times and shared their thoughts so I can grow and improve until the final version.

Thank you for the great editing and support from Paige.

Thank you for all the friends, family and supporters all over the World who read the first book "The Promise" and gave me positive energy to continue writing and finishing the journey I started.

Thank you Zsofia for the awesome cover. You are a true talent, inspiration and also the bestest friend I have to help me and support me in all my craziness.

At last, thank you to the person I am dedicating the book. My boyfriend, fiancé and soon husband to be. The person who proposed to me in Bali and the trip I will remember all my life. I am looking forward to our big day and sharing my vows with you.